Nothing Denied

Also by Jess Michaels

Nothing Denied

Jess Michaels

red

AVON

An Imprint of HarperCollinsPublishers

NOTHING DENIED. Copyright © 2010 by Jesse Petersen. All rights reserved. Printed in the United States of America. No part of this book may be used or reproduced in any manner whatsoever without written permission except in the case of brief quotations embodied in critical articles and reviews. For information address HarperCollins Publishers, 10 East 53rd Street, New York, NY 10022.

HarperCollins books may be purchased for educational, business, or sales promotional use. For information please write: Special Markets Department, HarperCollins Publishers, 10 East 53rd Street, New York, NY 10022.

FIRST EDITION

Library of Congress Cataloging-in-Publication Data is available upon request.

ISBN 978-0-06-165772-6

10 11 12 13 14   OV/RRD   10 9 8 7 6 5 4 3 2 1

To Michael,
for loving me in all my "J" name varieties.

Nothing Denied

Chapter One

"Jensen, I swear to the heavens that if one of those parcels so much as touches the drive, I will have you out on the street without a reference before supper," Beatrice Albright snapped as she shoved past the servant who was taking her packages down from the carriage after another afternoon of shopping.

The footman nodded nervously before he returned to his work. Smoothing her gown, Beatrice looked up at the tidy, fashionable house that rose up before her. God, how she dreaded returning to this place. It made her stomach ache just thinking about it.

It wasn't her actual residence that was the problem. Since her eldest sister had married an earl and her second eldest a duke, the family had not had to live in any kind of lowered status. In fact, the city manor was the nicest she had ever inhabited.

No, the *company* within was the problem in her home. The moment she walked through the door, she knew what she would find waiting for her: her mother, screeching and judging, and her youngest sister, Winifred, smiling and being sweet enough to rot Beatrice's teeth.

"Heaven save me," she muttered beneath her breath as she marched forward.

"I beg your pardon, miss?" the butler said as he stepped aside and allowed her entry.

Beatrice didn't answer, merely shot the man a dark glare and continued into the foyer where she began unbuttoning her coat.

The servant, accustomed to her varying moods, did not repeat the question, but merely held out a steady hand to take her hat and wrap. As she gave them over, he said, "Mrs. Albright is taking tea in the front parlor with Miss Winifred and Lady Rothschild."

At that, Beatrice stopped fussing with her gloves and turned on the man with a deepening frown. "Did you say that my sister is here? Miranda?"

The butler hesitated for a moment, not that Beatrice blamed him. Well, she *did* blame him, but some part of her also understood. One thing she prided herself on was her ability to raise the roof with a fit. Clearly, the butler was in anticipation of just that.

"Yes, Miss Beatrice. The Countess arrived shortly after your departure for the shops."

Beatrice huffed out her breath. "No doubt it was planned as such, so she could avoid seeing me."

She pretended not to feel a small flash of hurt at that statement. It wasn't that she *wanted* the kind of close relationship her two older sisters shared, or even the warm affection they seemed to have for Winnie. After all, she had spent a good part of the last few years pushing them away—why wouldn't they exclude her from their intimacy?

Thrusting her shoulders back, Beatrice tossed her gloves at the butler and made her way down the hall toward the front parlor. The door was open and from a few paces away, she heard female voices raised in spirited discussion. She hesitated, putting on the hard face she presented to the world, the one that wouldn't allow for hurt or vulnerability. Those were emotions she let no one else see.

"Oh, it isn't fair!" she heard her mother's harsh voice saying from within the room.

Beatrice could almost picture the pout lining her mother's round cheeks and the false tears sparkling in her eyes at whatever injustice she believed had been served against her. How Beatrice hated that sound, that face and the manipulations it hid.

"Are you certain you must take my little Winifred for the Season?" her mother continued.

Beatrice wrinkled her brow in confusion and came to a slow halt.

It was Miranda's voice that answered, as calm and infuriatingly soothing as always. "Do you not think it would be best, Mama? Winifred would join Ethan and me at Penelope's house party. She would very likely meet a wide variety of suitable gentlemen. I think she could have a very good chance of marrying well if we take her on as chaperones. Your hands are full enough with Beatrice."

"Yes," her mother mused with a rare lilt of reflection in her voice. "*Beatrice*. I suppose distancing Winifred from her sister *could* be better for her. The men might not be so intimidated. I would hate to end up with two unmarried daughters. One is humiliation enough for a mother."

At that, Beatrice staggered back until she brushed the wall behind her. Understanding had begun to dawn. It seemed she had been correct to assume Miranda had intended all along to come to the house while Beatrice was out. Her eldest sister had a scheme, one that involved marriage and an escape from their mother.

But not for her. No, Miranda was here to save Winifred. Pliable, weak-willed Winifred who wouldn't know a good match if he snuck her off to Gretna Green and compromised her.

Beatrice's hands shook as she marched forward once more and burst into the parlor. There her family sat, planning their treachery even while they appeared so innocent and kind.

Her mother had her usual place on the settee, Beatrice's

pretty, bland sister Winifred at her side like a little obedient dog.

Across from them was Miranda. Even Beatrice had to admit, though never out loud, that Miranda was probably the most beautiful of the Albright sisters. She practically glowed from within with happiness and contentment. It seemed she suffered no hardship whatsoever, or hadn't since she landed a most opportune match with the Earl of Rothschild, Ethan Hamon.

And Beatrice hated her for that, almost as much as she hated Miranda's happy marriage to a man she adored nearly as much as he worshipped her.

"Beatrice," Miranda said as she looked over toward the door. She got to her feet and her lips made a thin smile. "I didn't realize you were yet home."

"Oh, I should say not," Beatrice said, barely keeping her emotions in check as she dodged Miranda's hand of welcome. "In fact, I would wager my month's allowance that you were hoping not to see me at all today."

Miranda let out a small sigh that grated across Beatrice's nerves. How *dare* her sister be annoyed when it was Beatrice's life she was destroying? Did she not deserve her anger, her upset at the news she had just overheard in the hallway?

"What are you going on about?" Miranda said, innocent as a lamb as she retook her place on the settee and poured herself another cup of tea.

"Yes, dear," their mother stammered, but she was unable to meet Beatrice's eyes. "You seem upset."

Winifred was the only one who remained silent, her blue eyes darting downward in an expression of worry and submission.

"How could I not be upset when I overheard such villainy in the hallway?" Beatrice burst out, pacing across the room. "I know what you are planning!"

"You have always been so theatrical," Miranda said with another of her deep, put-upon sighs that so grated. "No one is plotting against you, Beatrice."

"No?" she barked out a humorless bark of laughter. "Is it not plotting against me when you offer to take Winifred under your wing and help her nab a rich husband while you leave me to rot here?"

Before Miranda could answer, Beatrice turned her attention on her mother. "Is it not treachery to speak of me as if I am a cross to bear?"

Their mother wrung her hands in her lap as Winnie sank down further in the settee cushions, but Miranda did not appear moved.

Her eldest sister arched a brow with a sniff of displeasure, "I realize this is difficult for you to understand, but not everything in this world is about *you*, Beatrice. There are many things that happen that have absolutely no bearing on your life. Ethan and I taking Winifred for the Season is one of those things."

"No bearing on my life? How can you say that?" Beatrice burst out, blinking in horror at the sudden tears that stung her eyes. She would not cry. She *never* cried, no matter how much something hurt. "Why are you taking Winnie, then?"

Miranda frowned. "It is the beginning of her fourth Season. We would like to afford her the chance to have a successful one."

Beatrice folded her arms. "And what about me, Miranda? I am in my seventh Season. *Seven*. And now you suggest that Winifred deserves some kind of special chance? Have you given up on me entirely, as Mama apparently has?"

Miranda shook her head and it was clear her frustration had reached its peak. "Admit it, you would not take anyone's help, even if it was offered. If you are in a seventh Season, it is not for my lack of assistance. You may not want to accept it, but your situation is of your own making. Your behavior, your lack of—"

Beatrice held up her hand to stop her sister, for she knew what Miranda would say, and unfortunately, most of it was true. She hated facing what she had done to create her own living hell.

"Do spare me. You and Penelope have regaled me quite enough times with a listing of my evils and shortcomings," she said, using her sharp tone to keep her sister from seeing how much the facts pained her.

Miranda got to her feet. "Beatrice—"

"No, you have made yourself completely clear," she said as she moved toward the door. "I see no reason to discuss this further. You are all determined to keep me an old maid and probably laugh at me when my fate is ultimately sealed, all while you hand Winifred an opportunity she will have no idea how to use. It is clear I will simply have to take my own future into my hands. Good day."

She stomped from the parlor, giving the door a hardy slam behind her that was quite satisfying. Down the hall she hurried, practically hurtling herself out the back doors and down the stairs into the garden. Once there, she slowed her pace and began to walk through the soft greens and bright colors. They did not soothe her, but at least outside in the sun she could breathe.

And think. Which was a double-edged sword, indeed.

Sucking in a deep breath, she considered what had just occurred. Miranda and Ethan would take Winifred away, and Penelope and her husband, Jeremy, would help them. With the support of a duke and an earl, and without the interference of their mother, Winifred would surely find a good match.

And that would mean that her younger sister would marry before her, making Beatrice even more of a laughingstock than she already was amongst those in Society. Beatrice could well picture the humiliation now as some of the young women she had cut over the years dangled their own husbands before her and mentioned their joy for Winifred.

The men would be no better. Over the years, Beatrice had turned down a great many of them . . . one of those she had rejected could very well take her sister's hand and she could do nothing but watch.

Watch and fall further into the hell that was her old maidenhood.

Oh yes, she knew she was an old maid. She was well aware that she had likely crushed any chance she had at finding love or friendship . . . or even just a man willing to settle for what others did not desire.

And yet somehow that had seemed bearable as long as she had a partner in her misery. But now Winifred would be gone and she would be alone.

Alone with their mother. Beatrice shuddered at the thought. Dorthea Albright would shower Beatrice with all of her attention, her wild moods, her incessant talking. There would be no escape, no one to foist her mother onto when it all became unbearable.

Beatrice shuddered as she considered the rest of her life. Soon she would receive fewer invitations, then none at all, save from her sisters. Her few remaining friends would fade away, leaving her at the mercy of her mother.

When that happened, she was certain she would go mad.

Beatrice flopped onto a bench in the center of the garden and massaged her temples. How could she escape this fate? There were few choices.

It was possible she could take a position as someone's ladies' maid or a governess, but she abhorred the idea of lowering herself in such a fashion. Aside from which, she had a tidy allowance thanks to her two brothers-in-law. Somehow she doubted the earl and the duke would let it be said that their kin had been forced into a life of servitude.

Which left her with but one option. To marry, as she had not been able to do for so long. She covered her eyes, rubbing hard on her temples as she considered the impossibility of her task. Because of a variety of circumstances, some of her own making and some not, no one had wanted her for years. Beatrice could not imagine finding someone who miraculously did so now.

Unless he was as undesirable as she was, herself.

She lifted her eyes at the thought. Could that work? Perhaps. Even if he wasn't ridiculously wealthy or scandalously handsome or cunningly intelligent as she had always hoped . . . any man she could catch would be a way out of her mother's house. A way to keep herself from being an utter fool in front of the entire *ton*.

And really, wasn't it her only option now?

Beatrice pushed to her feet and paced down the pathway. Yes, that had to be it. She would find the most undesirable man in the *ton* and she would make him hers. She *would* marry before this Season was finished.

Her sisters and her past and the consequences be damned.

Gareth Berenger, the Marquis of Highcroft, stood in his parlor staring at the letter he had already read at least a hundred times since he received it from his grandmother's solicitor three days prior. The words remained unchanged, but they continued to shock him every time he reviewed them.

"Have you managed to change your grandmother's deathbed wish by staring at the letter long enough?"

Gareth shook off his reverie and turned toward his best

friend, Vincent, Viscount Knighthill, with his best cold glare, the one that had made six maids quit over the years. Vincent merely feigned terror and poured himself a drink.

"If only I *could* change her final directive with my mind," Gareth finally groaned. "She never understood me. But then, no woman ever has."

Vincent rolled his eyes as he handed Gareth a tumbler. "Yes, you are so misunderstood, my friend. I know. It must be terrible to be rich and handsome and—"

"I possess several other qualities that are less desirable to women," Gareth interrupted as he downed his liquor in one gulp. The burning sensation did not alleviate his torment. "Which is precisely the problem. Grandmother's final wish was for me to remarry. Yet how can that be possible after the last time?"

Now Vincent's dark brown eyes softened with compassion. And pity, which Gareth flinched away from. "It wasn't your fault."

"It was and you know it," he snapped, hating himself more than ever. "You were there, you saw what I did."

His friend seemed on the verge of launching into the same argument they had been having for almost two years, but then he shook his head. Gareth all but sagged with relief. He was too exhausted to go over the past again and again.

"You know, you could always ignore her request if you fear the consequences so deeply," Vincent pointed out quietly. "Your grandmother has been buried for half a year, this letter was something she wrote months before that and arranged to be delivered once your mourning period was over. It isn't as if she will pursue you from the grave."

Gareth shut his eyes as the pain of his loss came crowding back into his body from the corner where he had banished it. He thought of his grandmother, a thousand memories at once, but all of them sharing one common element: her undying devotion and love to him when no one else had cared.

The idea of denying her one final desire simply because she would not be around to look at him in disapproval . . . well, it wasn't right.

"I cannot do that," Gareth said on a sigh. "Whether she is here to press me or not, I cannot in good conscience disregard her wishes. And her logic is very real, at any rate."

His friend nodded slowly. "You are the last male of your line. The last one who can create a son and continue the Highcroft line."

"If there is no marriage, there will be no heir." Gareth shrugged. "Is she not correct that it is my duty to prevent that from happening?"

"Yes, I suppose that is accurate." Vincent sighed. "It is bad luck to be the last of your line."

Gareth nodded silently. Bad luck, indeed. Sometimes it seemed his family had been cursed. Events of his life certainly supported such a foolish notion. He had once had two brothers, "spares" who might have saved him from this duty he did not wish to uphold.

But they had died within a year of each other, from two accidents. His mother had quickly followed, from a disease that had wasted her to near nothing before the end. Within a few years of her passing, his father had fallen ill of an apoplexy and gone to the grave beside her.

Before his twenty-first year, Gareth had seen his entire family decimated. And then there was his first wife, Laurel. She had been cold in the ground for two years, though he could not blame anyone but himself for that tragedy.

"Duty be damned, friend," Vincent said with a shake of his head. "It seems foolish to do something you want so little."

Gareth shrugged. "What I *want* makes no difference now."

Vincent's eyes went wide. "Then you are determined to re-enter Society."

It took every effort for Gareth to nod his head. "That is why we have come to London, isn't it?" A great sinking feeling settled over him, a weight on his shoulders that bogged him down. He could only hope it would not drown him in the end.

"Your task won't be easy," Vincent muttered, almost more to himself than to Gareth.

"No, my friend." Gareth paced to the window and looked out at the rainy afternoon. "I do not think it shall be. I may be the only rich, titled and reasonably handsome man that no one will choose to fight over."

Chapter Two

Beatrice straightened her spine and fought the urge to work her stiff jaw. Damn, but smiling all the time was painful. No wonder she had never bothered much with the mask.

But no, that was the wrong way to think. She could change her life this Season. She *would* change her life, no matter what the cost.

Across the room, she caught a gentleman watching her. Mr. Roger Westin, she thought his name was. He was only the third son of a marquis, and at one time she might have turned up her nose at him. But he had made a tidy fortune from some sort of business venture. He would do.

She made her forced smile wider and met his gaze . . . only to have him turn away with a shudder she recognized even from so far away. Her heart sank, but she refused to surrender to the panic rising in her chest.

Scanning the room, she found another gentleman who was away from the ladies. The Baronet Harker was older, yes, but he still had most of his teeth. And three small children who apparently needed a mother, if the gossip was to be believed. She shivered at the thought, but desperate times called for desperate measures. She met his gaze. But like Mr. Westin before him, Harker did not return her advances. In fact he backed away, as if she might come across the room and hit him with her shoe. Then he found the first person close to him and launched into a conversation so that he could politely ignore her.

The flush of embarrassment and terror began to fill Beatrice's cheeks, but before she could find a way to gracefully exit the room, her mother reached her elbow.

"Beneath you, both of them," she whispered, though her voice was anything but low, and several people close at hand tittered at the ridiculousness of her statement.

With cheeks burning hotter than ever, Beatrice clenched her fists tight at her sides. *Beneath* her. How many hundreds of times had her mother said that of perfectly decent men? Ones who might have been good matches for her? In the beginning, Beatrice had believed her mother, scorning those men.

Over time, the scorn had become a shield she held up. Now it was just second nature. The thought of losing that bitter exterior that protected her from anyone getting too close, from seeing any vulnerability, was quite frightening despite the fact that it damaged her at every turn, just as her mother's lofty expectations had.

"I thought you said that having an old maid as a daughter was a humiliation," Beatrice hissed, keeping her voice low so that no one heard. "Is that not what you confessed to Miranda when she offered to take Winifred away for the Season?"

She tried not to flinch as she thought of watching Winifred ride off in Miranda's fine carriage that very morning. Her sister had looked so happy to be free of their mother's prodding. Beatrice couldn't help but think that if she had not been so difficult, she, too, could have been free of her mother years ago, either by marriage or through some similar arrangement with her sisters.

"Yes, dear," her mother said, her blank stare meeting Beatrice's. "But that doesn't mean I wish for you to settle for just *any* man."

"An old maid like me cannot expect a gentleman with a title or grand fortune or . . ." Beatrice hesitated. "Teeth."

"Dearest—"

But she could not listen anymore. God, how she wanted an escape. And possibly a drink. And to hide from the crowd and their contempt for her. Perhaps she deserved it, for it was only a mirror of the feeling she had showered over others for so many years.

"I would like to take some air," Beatrice choked out. "I shall return in a moment."

Her mother opened her mouth to protest, but Beatrice did not wait. She fled across the room and through the open terrace doors into the damp, cool night. It was a temporary respite, of course. Escape from her mother was *always* temporary, but she had no choice but to take what she could get.

One way or another.

"Beatrice, is that you?"

Beatrice squeezed her eyes shut hard. She recognized the voice that had intruded on her moment of peace as the voice of her oldest . . . and virtually *only* remaining friend, Amelia Kinley.

"Yes, Amelia," she said with a sigh. "I am here."

Her friend stepped onto the dim terrace with a shiver. "There is a chill to the air, isn't there? What in the world are you doing out here?"

Beatrice shrugged. "It has not been a good night, I am afraid."

Her friend pursed her lips. "Yes, I assume not. The whole *ton* is abuzz about how Lord and Lady Rothschild have taken your sister under their wing this Season and swept her off to the exclusive gathering at the Duke and Duchess Kilgrath's in the country. Winifred will surely make a good match there."

Nostrils flaring, Beatrice calmed her natural reaction, which would have been to rip her friend to shreds and leave her crying. That would do her no good, no matter how enticing the idea was.

Instead, she sighed and turned to sarcasm rather than wrath. "Thank you, Amelia. Your observation is very helpful to me. After all, I am seven Seasons into my own old maidenhood. I wonder how many more I shall have before I am firmly and irretrievably on the shelf?"

Amelia tilted her head, clearly oblivious to Beatrice's true emotions. "Two more probably. Mama says no one can reach a decade of being out without becoming hopeless, no matter how pretty or rich or charming they are. And you are neither rich nor charming."

Beatrice stared. With most people, words like her friend's would be subtle knives intended to destroy, but Amelia was too empty for such sabotage and cruelty. In truth, her friend was so stupid that she didn't even realize she was being callous. The only reason Beatrice endured her was . . .

Well, in truth, there were few people left who allowed her presence. Beatrice had settled for Amelia, and now, staring at her vapid friend, she wondered if she would be forced to marry someone just like her. Perhaps her only remaining hope was a man too empty and stupid to recognize Beatrice's shortcomings.

It was almost too depressing to consider.

"Well, thank you, Amelia," she managed to grind out past clenched teeth. "I have much to think about thanks to your blunt words."

She pivoted, ready to stalk back into the ballroom and the waiting clutches of her mother, when Amelia grasped her arm and yanked her back.

"Oh, great God," her friend breathed.

Beatrice stared at Amelia, unaccustomed to any kind of real emotion from her empty little shell of a friend. Now Amelia's eyes were wide, her mouth made an "O" and she was actually trembling as she stared past Beatrice into the ballroom.

"What is it?" she asked.

Her friend shook her head. "Did you not see who just entered the ballroom?"

Beatrice turned and almost took a step back herself. The man who had just entered was not one she was personally familiar with, of course, but she knew him by reputation.

"Is that the Marquis of Highcroft?" she breathed.

Amelia nodded. "Gareth Berenger."

"Gareth," Beatrice repeated, staring at the man.

He remained across the room, so she could not discern individual features in any kind of depth, but she got a good sense of him nonetheless. He was tall, broad shouldered and very handsome. His dark hair was too long in front and curled around his forehead like he couldn't be bothered to give a damn about it. He had a strong, well-defined jaw that even from this distance appeared clenched and tense.

"Well, he is certainly as beautiful a man as gossip has labeled him," Beatrice said softly.

Her friend gasped beside her and let go of her arm suddenly. "Why should anyone care about that?"

"Everyone *always* cares about that," Beatrice said with a snort of laughter. "Please, you can do almost anything and get away with it if you are attractive. Especially men."

"That may be true most of the time," Amelia huffed. "But not in this case. My mama says a man like that will *never* be accepted back into good Society. Not after what he did. It doesn't matter how much money or beauty he brings out for everyone to see."

Beatrice narrowed her eyes as she looked once more at the specimen of a man who was moving across the floor. She couldn't help it. She moved toward the entrance to the room to see him better. Now she could tell that his eyes were as dark as the aura that surrounded him.

People stepped back as he moved among them, cutting a swath through the room as if he were a pariah. Of course, he was, wasn't he?

"Do you really think he would never find acceptance in Society?" she murmured. "Even with all the benefits he could bring to the lady he courted?"

"Never," Amelia hissed. "After all, everyone *knows* he murdered his wife."

The vein in Gareth's head was throbbing in time to the beat of the current song played by the orchestra. *One-two-three, one-two-three*, it pounded, making his vision blur and his stomach turn. Would this horrible night never end?

He paced from the edge of the dance floor and three young women all but tripped over one another to escape him, as if he would mangle one if he got within reach of her. It had been like that all night. Not one person beyond Vincent had spoken to him. They only stared.

In short, it was a complete disaster. Certainly Gareth had

not expected to find a match here in one night, but he had hoped for a better reaction. Perhaps a hint that he could overcome the gossip that surrounded him.

"This is terrible," he murmured as Vincent returned from fetching drinks.

His friend pursed his lips. "I won't lie and say that it is good. I think you might be able to make some inroads with the men at some point. A few seemed open to it in theory when I spoke to them throughout the night, but . . ."

"But the mamas and widows and chaperones are petrified," Gareth finished when his friend trailed off. "And the men might eventually do business with me or share port, but they wouldn't hand over their daughters. None of them will ever look beyond what they believe they know."

Vincent shrugged. "It will take time."

Gareth shut his eyes. If his friend was trying to be kind, it wasn't working. He wasn't daft. He could see that it would take more than time; it would take a miracle to overcome the rumors that he had killed his wife. And her family had only made those rumors worse. They blamed him publicly, and that only heightened the reaction of the mob.

"I need air," he muttered, and turned toward the terrace. Before he walked away, though, he noticed a young woman standing beside the punch table. She was alone, which was rare enough at these gatherings, and she was staring at him.

Her expression was not the sidelong glance of those who were whispering about him. And it wasn't one of the shuddering, sneaking looks of the debutantes who believed him to be a monster.

No, this young lady was casting him a look that was quite different. Interest, tempered by a little fear, yes. But mostly appraising.

"Who is that?" Gareth asked with a subtle motion of his hand in her direction. "The blonde lady who is watching me so carefully."

To his surprise, it was his friend who shivered when he followed Gareth's motion and looked upon the staring woman in question. "Beatrice Albright is her name. They call her—"

"The shrew," Gareth interrupted. "Yes, I recall her from the days before my marriage. She had quite the reputation for being a . . ." He stopped. Cursing in the middle of the ball would do him no good. "Well, they say she is difficult."

"There is another word for it, friend," Vincent said as he downed his drink.

Gareth smiled and it felt good for the first time this long, horrible night. "And did she ever marry?" he asked, casting his attention to the young lady a second time.

"Good God, no!" his friend burst out. "Who would ever have her after all these years?"

Gareth tilted his head. Shrew or not, she was beautiful, there was no denying that. Her thick blond hair was bound up at the nape of her neck and interesting tendrils bounced down around her breasts from the pretty style. She was wearing a fine gown made from some kind of delicate blue silk that matched the cornflower paleness of her eyes. If one went by surface appearance alone, one would think her quite malleable and pretty.

A deeper look, however, would correct that assumption. A haughty turn to her full lips, a snap of stubbornness to her eyes, yes, it was clear that this was a woman who would never bend. Not unless broken properly. An unexpected thrill coursed through him at the thought of doing just that. Turning her from shrew to mewling kitten.

Beatrice was still staring and he caught her glance and held there, waiting for her to turn away. Instead she folded her arms and stared right back. He almost laughed out loud. She had no idea just how much she was taunting him. Just how dangerous she was making him feel.

Suddenly an older woman appeared at her elbow and Beatrice turned away to face her.

"Still, she is beautiful," Gareth muttered as he broke away from her siren's spell and moved toward the terrace door.

"Trust me, friend," Vincent said as he followed. "No one wants her."

"Yes," Gareth muttered. "Just as no one wants me."

At a young age, Beatrice had learned to block out her mother's never-ending chatter. Sometimes that ability was the only thing to keep her sane, especially when her mother had turned all her attention on Beatrice and her drive to marry her to someone better than even her sisters had found.

Tonight, she silently cherished her ability to make her

mother's voice fade, as Dorthea Albright was wildly chatter-
ing about the ball they had just returned from at such a speed
that it would have made Beatrice's head spin if she actually
attended. Instead, she insulated herself in her own thoughts
as she paced the floor of the parlor.

Tonight had been a disaster. Somehow, in her heart she had
retained a little hope that, if she put some small effort into
her behavior, she could regain some of the interest of those
around her. She had pictured, however vaguely, that the more
stupid men of the *ton*, or the ones with few prospects, might
forget her reputation if she simply forced a smile and batted
her eyelashes.

It hadn't worked and it was perfectly clear that bridges had
not just been burned over the years, but obliterated by both
her own behavior and her mother's. No one would have her
. . . and even if she found someone who would, well, she shuddered at the kind of man he might be, to overlook the shortcomings that kept others away.

Shutting her eyes, Beatrice rested her forehead against the
cold glass of the window before her. It eased the ache a fraction and she sighed as she relaxed a little. Her mind slowed
and she found it conjuring other images from the evening's
gathering.

Ones of the Marquis of Highcroft.

He might have been the only person at tonight's ball to
have a worse experience than she had. While people shunned
her ever so subtly, with him it had been utter rejection—
terror, even. It was rare that someone with wealth, position

and such attractiveness could not have his sins overlooked, but it seemed the marquis had struck upon that odd combination that made all his advantages fade in comparison to the rumors that swirled around him.

In some ways, she and the marquis were the same. They were both utterly rejected, their hope of overcoming the past almost nonexistent.

Beatrice opened her eyes and stared out at the darkened street. Hadn't she vowed she would pursue a man no one else wanted? Of course, she hadn't been picturing a potential murderer when she made that vow to marry, and the consequences of her choice be damned.

She looked over her shoulder to find her mother still speaking. Girding herself for what she was about to do, she faced her mother and interrupted.

"Mama, all the talk was of the Marquis of Highcroft this evening. I have not seen him out in company since his wife's death."

Her mother's lips pursed. "Yes, dear, I was just speaking of the marquis. Were you not attending?"

Beatrice flinched. "Yes, of course, I only have a slight ache in my head, I was momentarily distracted."

The lie appeased her mother, as all lies did, and Dorthea launched into another long string of sentences without drawing breath. "I was shocked Lady Wilkinshire invited him at all, what with his reputation, but I believe they may have had some kind of friendship in the past, so perhaps he traded on that connection. Scoundrel!"

Beatrice arched a brow. Even the most innocent debutante knew that Lady Wilkinshire was a wild thing, taking great pride in her affairs since she had gifted her elderly husband with his heir and two male spares. Beatrice could only imagine what kind of "friendship" her ladyship might have once had with the handsome marquis. Perhaps even continued to have.

Her mother continued, "Either way, if he thought coming to her ball would make him acceptable, he was mistaken."

"Yes, he was shunned with greater force than even I was," Beatrice mused with a bitterness she could not cease.

Her mother's frown deepened, but then she seemed to push aside whatever negative thoughts had passed her mind. "Everyone else's sins fade in the face of his, my dear. The things he did!"

"His wife's death, you mean," Beatrice said, picturing the man again. He didn't look like she would picture a murderer would. "Do you think those whispers are true? *Did* he kill her?"

She found herself holding her breath as her mother took a rare moment of quiet contemplation. Then she shrugged one shoulder. "In truth, no one knows. Speculations abound, though. And his wife's family has been quite vocal in their accusations."

Beatrice rolled her eyes. The *ton* could speculate on anything! It didn't make it true. She, herself, had started rumors that spun out of control. A little guilt tugged at her, but she pushed it away. There was no use dwelling on all the things she had done. She had to focus on the future. On changing . . . at least enough to catch a man.

"Is there evidence that he might have done her a harm?" she asked.

Dorthea blinked. "Evidence? It is no secret they were not happy."

Beatrice wrinkled her brow. Great God, *she* wasn't happy. That didn't mean she was about to go killing someone.

"But it isn't certain," she mused.

Her mother stared at her. "I suppose not. But why take the chance?"

For the first time in a long time, Beatrice looked at her mother with begrudging respect. Of course Dorthea was right. With so much rumor and innuendo about the man, a girl would be foolish to risk herself, especially if she had any other prospects left.

Certainly, Beatrice wasn't so low that she had to pursue a potential killer just to escape her mother's influence. No, she would just continue her new plan. At the next ball, she would force herself to be kind and smile, and eventually it *would* fool some man into paying her attention.

She crossed to the bell and rang for a servant. When a footman arrived, she snapped, "Fetch the invitations for the rest of the week."

The footman actually stepped back a long pace and his face paled slightly. "Miss, er, well—"

Beatrice tilted her head. "What is it, man? Spit it out."

"There are no invitations," the man said, his voice trembling.

Beatrice stared at him for a long moment before she spun on her mother. "*No invitations?*"

Her mother clutched her fingers before her, genuine distress filling her normally vapid expression. "I had hoped a few would come tonight while we were out."

Beatrice's hands began to shake. "This cannot be true. We must have been invited to something in the next few days. A tea, a musicale, a ball. Something!"

Her mother shook her head. "It seems that now that Winifred is out of the house and Miranda and Penelope are in the countryside, there are no invitations."

Beatrice's stomach turned in one nauseating flop and it took everything in her not to scream. So this was it. A moment she had thought she had another year . . . perhaps two . . . before she had to face it. But it was unexpectedly and awfully here.

Finally, all her worst behavior had come to its ultimate end, the one she could almost admit she deserved in the deepest parts of her soul. She had been utterly and completely shunned by Society. Her life as she knew it was over.

Chapter Three

Beatrice smoothed her dress as she stepped out of Miranda and Ethan's opera box into the crowd that swirled about during intermission. A few cast side glances at her as they stood in their insular groups, chatting about mundane topics, but it was clear that she no longer existed to most.

Desperation clawed at her as she fully felt the consequences of all she had done over the years, but she shoved it down deep within her. Especially now, there was no room in her life for such weakness. She was here for a purpose and she intended to complete it.

After she got rid of her mother.

"Mama, is that not Lady Briarwood?" she whispered.

Her mother lifted on the balls of her feet to peer over the

crowd and her eyes lit up. "It is! I do wish to say hello to my old friend."

Beatrice tilted her head as pity rushed through her. Sometimes, in these little moments, she saw her mother without the blinders of her own frustration, and Dorthea Albright made a pathetic picture, indeed. A lady who had lost everything, including some small part of her mind, and her mother had always been desperate to recapture some part of her youth.

Beatrice could almost sympathize, even while she prayed she wouldn't one day be just like the woman before her, anxious to recover what she had lost in any way possible.

"Why don't you say hello," she said, her voice gentler. "I think I see Amelia over there. We shall meet back at the box when intermission is over."

Her mother was already waving her off as she moved toward one of the few ladies who still made an attempt to be kind to her. Beatrice heaved a sigh of relief. There was one obstacle cleared away. And since Amelia and her family were not truly there, that meant she was free for at least a quarter of an hour.

She looked around the milling crowd with careful vigilance. Somewhere here, the Marquis of Highcroft was in attendance. She had made certain of that before she begged her mother to use her brother-in-law's box for the night. Now she just had to find him in the crowd.

It didn't take long, for the man stood out like some kind of dark angel. In the distance she caught sight of him, leaning against a pillar with an unlit cigar in his fingers. He was making a slow, steady perusal of those around him, like a cat stalking prey. And he was alone, which made this the perfect time for her to approach.

Her heart pounded, rushing blood to her ears and making her a little lightheaded as she advanced on him. She stopped just a pace or two before him and looked up at him. Doubts and questions flashed through her mind, but with difficulty she shook them away.

"Good evening," she said, very pleased that her tone sounded just as haughty as it always did. There was no use showing fear to this man.

One dark brow quirked as the marquis stared down at her and then slowly straightened up. "Good evening."

Now Beatrice squirmed just a bit. What she was doing was utterly against protocol. One did not approach a strange man with such boldness. She wasn't entirely clear on what she should do now.

"I assume you know who I am," he said, breaking the silence she had not yet filled.

She nodded. "Yes. You are Gareth Berenger, the Marquis of Highcroft."

He inclined his head slightly. "And *you* are Beatrice Albright."

She frowned. Damn, she had held out some small hope that he would be unaware of her, allowing her to reveal her problem with reputation in the manner of her choosing. But he knew her name, which meant he had probably heard as many stories about her as she had about him.

Still, she pressed on, determined to remain on this course. "It appears our reputations have preceded us."

For the first time the hint of a smile tilted his full lips and Beatrice stared despite herself. He really was a handsome man, and those lips were remarkably full. A wild image of him kissing her suddenly entered her mind and she shoved it aside with a gasp.

"Are you quite all right?" he asked, stepping toward her.

She wanted to step away, to draw back from the darkness and the heat that seemed to radiate from his body. But she forced herself to stand her ground. She did not bend for any man. Even this one.

"I'm very fine, thank you." She arched a brow.

Again that smile tilted his lips, but now it was wolfish. "Indeed you are."

She blinked. Was that flirtation? Dear Lord, she hardly recognized it anymore, it had been so long.

Or perhaps he was mocking her.

"If you know me, then you must have heard the rumors about me," she said, moving forward to the matter at hand.

His brow arched. "Indeed, and you surely know of my reputation, as well."

She nodded. "The things they say about *me* are true."

A burst of laughter escaped his lips and drew the attention of a few people around them. Beatrice sent the closest group a glare that made them all look away again.

Vultures.

"Are they now, Miss Albright?" he asked. "Are you sure you want to admit to that?"

"Why shouldn't I? I know what I am. I *am* difficult. I am snobbish. I am . . . am . . . "

"A bitch?" he asked.

She flinched at his blunt use of the vulgar term she knew was whispered behind her back. It was her own fault that he said it. She had been bold, why would he not be?

"Perhaps," she said with a shrug.

"Such honesty is not the norm with ladies of your stature, my dear," he said. "I do not know whether to admire it or be wary of its cost."

"There is no cost," she said swiftly, watching his mouth move with increasing fascination. "Except that I hope my honesty will inspire yours in return. You see, Lord Highcroft, I wanted to know if—"

She broke off. How exactly did one ask such a delicate question? Now that she was standing with him and he was so tall and so focused on her, the prudence of this course of action seemed less clear to her.

"Are you asking if the rumors about me are also true?" he asked.

She nodded, relieved he had voiced what she could not. "Would I be in danger if we weren't surrounded by this crowd?"

He inched ever closer, almost until their bodies touched. She could smell him now, an interesting combination of sandalwood and smoke and something warm and enticing that she couldn't place. She breathed it in and resisted the urge to sigh in response.

"Perhaps you would be, Miss Albright, though not in the manner you may be imagining."

He smiled, but it was feral, not friendly. Her heart began to race as his shadow closed over her, but she couldn't look away and she couldn't move.

"Beatrice!"

She shook her head as her name pierced through the fog around her. She turned toward the voice and was surprised to see her sister Penelope's husband crossing through the crowd toward her. By his purposeful gate and dark scowl, Jeremy Vaughn, Duke of Kilgrath was not pleased.

He caught her arm and she turned to see what Gareth's reaction to this interruption was, but to her surprise, he was already gone. She refocused on Jeremy.

"Release me at once!"

"I shall not," he hissed as he hauled her down the corridor to the curtain before Miranda and Ethan's box. "What do you think you're doing?"

Beatrice blinked her eyes innocently. "I was enjoying the opera until someone manhandled me like a brute."

Jeremy squeezed his eyes shut and Beatrice thought he might have murmured a curse beneath his breath before he snapped, "With the company you were keeping, you are lucky you were only manhandled."

"I don't know what you mean," she lied.

"You were with Gareth Berenger!"

She shook his hand away and folded her arms. "And *you* are supposed to be in the country with my sisters, trying to find a match for perfect little Winifred, not here spying on me, the sister everyone hates."

Jeremy leaned back in surprise at the strength of her response.

"I had a bit of business to finish in London before I joined the party." He looked at her and his expression softened. She recognized the look as pity and flinched back from it. "Beatrice—"

She cut him off with a glare. "Please don't pretend that any of you give a damn about me."

"Everyone gives a damn about you," he whispered, but it was clear his patience was at an end. "For God's sake, you know what people say about the marquis, why would you speak to him without a chaperone?"

"First off, people say a great many things that are not true, Jeremy. *You* should know that," Beatrice began. "And it wasn't as if I was alone with the marquis."

At least not yet.

He frowned, but she could see he had no retort to either of her defenses.

"You may be correct that what people say isn't true," he said finally. "I have no idea what Gareth Berenger is or isn't or what he did or didn't do. However, I *do* know that it would be prudent of you to stay clear of him. There are a great many questions surrounding him that could have very dangerous answers."

Beatrice turned away and wrenched the curtain aside. "Well, I've been left with very little choice, haven't I? Winifred is being taken care of, but I must fend for myself."

She sent him one last glance before she entered the box and screeched the curtain shut behind her.

Gareth dug his heels into his mare's sides and urged her forward at a faster pace. The wind blew through his hair as they pounded down a twisting path through Hyde Park and for the first time since his return to London, he felt free. A ride had always been a good way to solve his problems, wherever he was or whatever they were.

Today, however, one thought kept returning to his mind. An image of Beatrice Albright in the moment before her brother-in-law interrupted them at the opera. In that one brief instant, her walls of steel and venom had come tumbling down and he had seen a vulnerability that called to his deepest and darkest self.

She could be tamed. He had seen it. And the taming would be such a pleasure, indeed.

Beyond that immediate sexual attraction he had so surprisingly felt, he had also been impressed by the girl's boldness. Everyone whispered about him, but there was only mock bravery in staying behind one's fan and wondering. No one had ever had the gall to simply walk up to him and ask him point-blank if he was a murderer.

And yet one little unchaperoned shrew of a girl had. And if she had trembled, it was very little. No, she had looked him right in the eye and challenged him, all the while throwing the words that had been whispered about *her* out in the open with no excuses or blushes.

Yes, that sort of boldness interested him on a variety of levels. Yet it changed nothing. On one of the first nights after his arrival in London, his former lover Lady Wilkinshire had invited him to her soiree, but he had no illusions that she had done so to help him. No, she liked to shock and she liked to flaunt her affairs like the one they had briefly shared before he married Laurel.

At any rate, that single appearance in good company had done him no good. No invitations had been forthcoming since. He had been relegated to public events like the previous evening's opera or the daily deluge of Hyde Park to make his appearances. He was left with only the slender hope that someone of importance would take interest in or pity on him and ask him to attend a gathering.

This was not a situation he was accustomed to, waiting for the approval of others. He was a man of power. He did not like to leave his fate in the fickle hands of others. And yet he had lost his choices, lost his reputation, lost everything, the moment Laurel landed at the bottom of that staircase, her life snuffed out in a horrible instant.

Pulling his horse to a stop and tethering her on a nearby tree, Gareth paced a short distance down the path. Those thoughts, those memories of his wife, remained as disturbing as the day they had occurred. He would give anything to find a way to forget.

"Lord Highcroft!"

Gareth froze as a female voice called out to him from behind. He turned and watched as the very woman he had been contemplating before his thoughts turned maudlin pulled her own filly to a stop and hopped down gracefully.

Beatrice Albright was dressed in a smart riding habit that pulled tight across the smooth curve of her breasts and cinched around the small expanse of her waist. As her clothing had the first night he saw her, the blue color of her frock matched her eyes, making their pale color jump out from her flushed cheeks. Her hair was bound up beneath a cap, but little locks of it peeked out, teasing him with honey softness.

"Miss Albright," he managed to say, moving toward her. "It seems we are thrown into each other's path again, though I cannot say that I am unhappy to see you."

She arched a brow and that challenging look made his loins ache. She probably had no idea the effect she had, which made it all the better.

"Well, I must first admit that I followed you today, my lord," she said, though she did not look ashamed. "We were interrupted last night and I greatly wish to finish our conversation."

He smiled. "Ah, Miss Albright, I must say you are the most direct lady I have met in a long while. It is quite refreshing."

Her eyes narrowed as she stared at him, almost as if she were trying to determine whether he was mocking her or not. Finally, she shrugged one shoulder.

"Unfortunately, that is my problem. You see, most men don't find my directness to be an asset. In fact, they despise my forward, sharp nature. And *that* is my purpose for following you today."

He folded his arms. "To tell me that most men don't like you?"

She huffed out her breath. "You do delight in being difficult, don't you?"

The moment she said it, her face paled a shade and she squeezed her eyes shut hard. Gareth watched in wonder as she calmed herself and when she looked at him again, he recognized the mask that she had put on. She smiled, but it wasn't real. She softened her angles, making her far less interesting, in his estimation.

"I apologize, my tongue sometimes has its own mind."

Gareth smothered a low groan. He could too easily imagine what sorts of things her tongue could do if she allowed the right teacher to show her the way.

"Is there something wrong?" she asked, tilting her head in the first show of genuine concern he had ever seen her make. "You made a funny sound just then."

"No, clearing my throat," he lied. "Miss Albright, it has become abundantly clear that you sought me out today in order to discuss something with me. Why don't we do so?"

She almost sagged in relief that she would not have to keep up the girlish, simpering mask. Straightening her shoulders, she met his eyes directly and began to speak.

"You are correct, my lord. Although we arrived to the places we are today in very different ways, I believe you and I are in a similar circumstance."

"And what circumstance is that, my dear?"

She pursed her lips at the endearment, but continued, "Last night we spoke of the fact that we both have a reputation that turns the *ton* away from us. A reputation that will be difficult, if not impossible to overcome, and yet we both wish to do so. I believe you may want to marry again, am I wrong in that assumption?"

Gareth shrugged. *Want* might be a strong word, but there was no need correcting her. "Yes, I have come to London in the hopes that I might eventually find a bride. I have an obligation to do so."

"And I need a husband for . . . well, for a variety of reasons." She drew a breath and for the first time Gareth saw her nervousness before she proceeded. "It is likely neither of us will be able to fulfill our goals alone, so I propose we join forces. My lord, what if we were to marry each other?"

Chapter Four

The Marquis of Highcroft did not seem to be the kind of man who shocked easily. In fact, before his marriage and his wife's untimely death, Beatrice had some vague recollections that he had been known for shocking others. So when he drew back, eyes wide and mouth open, she actually felt a swell of pride. Whether or not he took her offer, he would certainly never forget her.

And that actually seemed like a success.

"Are you asking for my hand in marriage?" he asked after a few long seconds of silence.

She rolled her eyes. "I suppose it is something like that, though I prefer to call it something far less silly and romantic. I am making you a business offer."

After another breath of shocked silence, he shook his head. "My dear, where is your chaperone?"

Beatrice blinked in confusion. "I beg your pardon?"

He motioned around him wildly. "Clearly, you are not safe to be left unattended if you run around making marriage proposals to men you have met all of two times."

Beatrice narrowed her gaze. There was nothing she hated more than the arrogance of a man who did not understand she had her own mind and was perfectly capable of using it. Still, she had to be careful not to lose her temper, for it had gotten her in trouble more than once.

"I came to the park with a friend and her mother," she said through grinding teeth. "However, they were distracted and I managed to slip away when I saw you."

"Do you not think they will notice your absence and make search? What will they say when they find us alone together?"

Beatrice tightened her jaw. "In all honesty, Amelia's mother is probably just as happy to be rid of me."

"Is that so?" he drawled as he folded his arms. "And why is that?"

She sighed heavily. "As I said, I do not have prospects and I tend to ruin those of the people around me. Now please, be serious and let us discuss my proposal."

He shook his head and continued to stare at her like she was some kind of alien creature. "I do not know how you can put the word *serious* in the same sentence as one referring to this ridiculous offer you are making."

Panic rose up in Beatrice's chest, but she shoved it back.

"And why not? You cannot deny that I speak the truth. *No one* wishes to marry you, my lord. In fact, I have heard whispers that those in our sphere do not even want you in their homes. Your attempts at reentering Society have been limited to appearances in public places like the opera last night or today in Hyde Park. Am I wrong?"

To her surprise, Highcroft merely tilted his head in acquiescence. He was staring at her still, but his expression had begun to transform from one of utter horror and shock to a look of interest. She clung to the slender reed of hope it gave her and continued.

"How do you think you will ever make a match if no one will so much as speak to you?" She shrugged. "It seems perfectly reasonable to me that you would consider turning to another person who was just as shunned by Society."

"And that person is you?" he asked.

She nodded, fighting to keep from blushing in humiliation. "Yes. Trust that there is no woman anyone wants less. But I still believe we could both benefit greatly from a match."

He simply stared at her when she was silent to allow him to speak. She shifted uncomfortably.

"It isn't as if I'm some servant grasping for a higher place," she explained. "My father was a gentleman and my brothers-in-law are both of highly elevated status."

To her great relief, he nodded. "Indeed, that is true. My objection is not due to your lack of breeding, Miss Albright."

She blinked. He could not say no. She had to find a way to stop him from refusing. No matter what.

"Then what *is* your objection?"

He hesitated then a low chuckle reverberated from his lips. The sound of it curled up her spine and made her body tingle in a strange and powerful way. She sucked in a breath and tried to make it stop.

"I object because I don't think you really know what you are asking for, little girl."

The tingles she had been trying to suppress fled at his arrogance. She placed a hand on each hip and glared at him.

"Don't you call me that. You have no idea who I am or what I know or what I've seen." Her reminders to stay calm left her mind in an instant. "You are such a typical, arrogant lord, aren't you? You pretend to be more, that you lurk behind this mysterious, alluring shadow, but you still don't see anyone but yourself. I think you might be the most—"

She didn't get a chance to finish. Not when Gareth grasped her wrist, hauled her against his chest and crushed his mouth to hers in a fashion that was anything but gentle or coaxing.

No, he devoured her. It wasn't exactly the first kiss Beatrice had imagined when she allowed herself such flights of fancy. And yet the bruising, punishing pressure on her lips lit a fire inside of her that quickly rose to terrifying heights. She felt hot and yet shivery all at once, her legs shook, her nipples ached, her sheath clenched.

Even as an innocent with only the words whispered in back rooms about what would happen when a man and woman joined together, she felt the promise in his kiss. When he pressed his tongue past her lips and assaulted the cavern of her mouth, she pictured the way he might breach her body with his. He would not be gentle, but he would bring her pleasure. He would *force* her pleasure and control it.

Which was a rather terrifying thought.

Suddenly he yanked away from her, letting her stagger back without any gentlemanly offer of assistance. She lifted a hand to her hot, throbbing lips and stared at him in stunned silence.

"Now then, do you still think you might like to marry me?" he asked, his breath coming in pants.

She stared at him, a faint twinge of disappointment troubling her. It appeared he hadn't kissed her out of desire, but as some kind of tactic to put her off her plan.

"Was *that* meant to frighten me, my lord?" She laughed and hoped it sounded stronger than she felt. "It did not. My offer still stands. Are you man enough to take it and resolve both our problems?"

He watched her for a long, charged moment and then he began to laugh. "Oh yes, breaking you would be a delight."

She cocked her head. She wasn't sure she liked the idea of being broken, even though the tone he used when he said it seemed to cut through her like a heated knife.

"My dear, perhaps you do not know this, but my lowered reputation does not only involve my wife's—" He broke off and shook his head. "Well, it doesn't just involve the rumors around her death. You see, even before I married, even before I became infamous, I was considered somewhat of a liability for some of the more attentive families. Do you know why?"

She shook her head, struck momentarily dumb by the mesmerizing way he was moving toward her. Like she was a helpless mouse and he a snake. No one ever treated her like that. Most men were ninnies around her, easily frightened away by her sharp tongue.

"Well, you see I have certain *passions* . . . certain *proclivities* when it comes to women. And I've learned through harsh experience that any woman who calls me husband must be able to bear those things or else our marriage will be a very unhappy one, indeed." He reached out and traced a finger down her cheek. "You are a strong-willed woman, Beatrice. You might not like what marrying and bedding with me would entail."

She shivered as his fingers moved to her throat, tracing the curve there before he found the lacy slope of her gown's neckline and teased his fingers just beneath the surface. She realized she should flinch away, but she couldn't. His touch was like liquid lightning. All heat and explosive energy that brought a throbbing urgency to her body.

"What are you saying?" she whispered, hating her broken voice, hating the way her skin flushed and gave away her secret pleasure at his forward, distasteful display.

"I will never again take a woman for a bride who could not participate in my activities." He smiled, but it was thin. "So if you want to form a union with me, I am proposing a test."

"A . . . a test?" she repeated stupidly, still captivated by his warm touch.

He nodded. "An affair."

Beatrice found herself stepping backward as the utter shock of what he was suggesting hit her. She stared at him as she tried to muster indignation, disgust, outright rage . . .

Only none of those things rose up in her. In fact, the reactions that did come were not what she expected and they made her cheeks flush.

Interest. Titillation. And worst of all, desire.

If other women and their families shied away from whatever sexual interests he had, they must be terrible, indeed, and yet she couldn't help but long to know more. To experience *some* kind of passion. It had been so long since any man showed an interest in her that she had almost forgotten what heated regard felt like.

That memory that had been brought back immediately when Gareth kissed her. In that passionate moment she had felt wanted, desirable . . . and owned in a way she hadn't expected.

"An affair," she whispered.

He shrugged. "I will understand when you say no. After all, it isn't an arrangement most women of your station would ever accept, and with very good reason."

Beatrice's eyes narrowed as she observed the boredom in his posture and the expectation in his eyes. He thought his suggestion would frighten her away, keep her from pursuing the only course of action left open to her.

Well, he clearly didn't fully understand her straits. She had to marry at any cost. She couldn't afford to refuse this chance, but she *could* negotiate terms.

"I'm not afraid of you, no matter how you try to manipulate me," she said, moving closer even as her trembling body screamed at her to run away, far and fast. "Now tell me, sir, is your offer a genuine one or are you only trying to put me off?"

He leaned in closer. "Trust me, sweetling, I don't ask someone to be my lover unless I mean it."

A swell of relief filled her, but she shoved it aside. She couldn't just accept his stunning proposal without delving deeper into the particulars.

"I want to be certain I understand you," she said, folding her arms. The action brought his gaze down to her breasts and she started as he stared with a feral smile. He was ogling her . . . and she rather liked it.

"Do continue," he pressed, arching a brow. "What are you uncertain of?"

She shook off her discomfort. "You are saying that if I engaged in an affair with you and you felt I could stand th—the lifestyle you are apparently involved in, you would wed me?"

He nodded. "Yes. If we were a good match in bed, you are correct that a marriage between us would solve both our problems."

Silent joy flooded her. She was so close to her objective now, there was no turning back.

"And how long would you expect me to conduct an affair with you before you fulfilled your promise to marry me?"

He tilted his head as if examining her closer. "I think we would both know within a fortnight whether we were compatible. If we came to terms, we could be married within a few days of that time."

She nodded. Counting in travel time and unexpected contingencies, she could be married within a month if he was to be trusted. How bewitching that prospect was, and all it would entail was a bit of faith on her part.

And yet that was the hardest thing to offer. Faith was so easily crushed, as she well knew.

Piercing him with a pointed stare, she said, "My only concern is what will happen if you go back on what you promise. I think I can endure anything you ask of me, but what if you change your mind at the end of the affair? What if you use me, take my virtue and then refuse to marry me?"

He drew back and it was genuine offense that flickered in his stare. "That would be the height of dishonor, Miss Albright. I may be many things, but a cad is not one of them."

"I'm certain no cad has ever denied his true colors," she snapped, her tone dripping sarcasm. "You may tell me your word is your bond all day, however it doesn't change the fact that in our current positions, you hold all the power and I hold all the risk."

He stared at her a long, heated moment, as if her words had conjured up some image that pleased and aroused him. She found herself drawn in by his stare, held captive by how focused he had become on her. His ability to hold her sway wasn't one she had experienced before, and truth be told it frightened her a little.

And yet what choice did she have?

"I suppose you are correct that you're risking the greater consequence," he finally said when the silence had seemed to stretch out forever. "If it would make you feel better, I can have a contract drawn up between us. Something that provides you with a more than handsome living should I go back on my word. One way or another, when we were finished, you would have your independence whether by your marriage to me or via a monetary settlement."

Beatrice's lips pursed as she considered Gareth's bargain in full detail. She considered her situation first and foremost. Whatever she did, it was highly unlikely that she could change the *ton*'s view of her. The lack of invitations this week was only the first step down the road to fully becoming an old maid. And she could smile or simper or pretend to be a fragile dove all she wanted, but too many had seen her true character. The men who didn't know her would be warned away, the women would enjoy her downfall because she had cut them down over the years.

Because of her own behavior, any bargaining chips she had gained from her sisters' good marriages or the respected quality of her father's name had long been crushed. Certainly, her virginity was not even an issue. Not since no man could see past her poor conduct and overbearing mother.

If remaining chaste would not help her, why should she not use her body in a different way to obtain her freedom? It didn't mean she would surrender her soul or her heart. Her body would become a commodity and in the end she would win what she desired most.

Wasn't that worth the sacrifice? Especially when considering the alternative.

"If you had such an agreement written up, I would consider what you have asked of me," she finally agreed, hiding her shaking hands behind her back. "And if you made every effort to protect whatever reputation I might have left."

He drew back. "You surprise me, Miss Albright. I admit I thought you were bluffing."

Her eyes narrowed. "Well, you do not know me at all, my lord."

He smiled. "And yet it seems I'll soon know you most intimately."

When he laughed, her skin tightened and her body heated, but she did not respond. She wouldn't give him the satisfaction.

He arched a brow. "If we were to make this arrangement, it would have to take place at my estate half a day's journey west of London. I can promise you that it is quite secluded despite its proximity to the city and my staff is trustworthy to a fault. No one would need know what we did together, as long as you could escape your mother and find a way to journey unattended to me."

Beatrice twisted her mouth. That was the one contingency she had not considered. Escape from her mother would not be an easy task. Beatrice could pretend an invitation from Amelia to the country, but her mother could not stand to be left out of anything. She would insist on coming along and ruin everything.

Unless . . .

"I might need your help with removing my mother from the equation," Beatrice said with a sudden smile. "Do you think you could help me have a letter posted as if it were from another place?"

Gareth nodded. "I believe that would be possible. But will that truly help your situation?"

"If I write the proper letter, she will abandon me with ease." Her smile wavered. "You see, my lord, I know exactly how my family functions. All I must do is manipulate my mother's desire to be important."

He nodded after a moment's consideration. "Then it seems we have come to an accord."

Beatrice swallowed, for the first time realizing exactly what it was she had agreed to. "Yes, it seems we have."

She held out a hand to shake on the bargain, but instead he drew her closer. She felt his hot breath on her skin, his hand was heavy as it slipped around her back and settled just above her bottom in a most inappropriate and exciting way. He molded her body to his and she felt the hard length of his erection against her belly as he stared down at her.

"We should kiss on it, Miss Albright. It is the best way to seal a deal of this nature."

She swallowed. The first time he had kissed her, she hadn't had room or time to ponder what would happen. Now he moved his mouth to hers with seductive slowness and she could hardly breathe as she awaited his touch.

But he didn't kiss her lips. Instead, his mouth found the curve of her throat and his tongue teased out to drag along the line of her pulse. To her shock, Beatrice found herself arching against him as he sucked the tender column of her skin. Strange, powerful sensations overwhelmed her, making her legs shake as his mouth glided ever lower.

But finally, he pulled away.

"I look forward to doing that again when you have fewer layers." With a grin, he turned away. "I'll speak to you very soon, Miss Albright. And I look forward with great anticipation to seeing you in my home. And my bed."

With those parting words, he was gone, back on his horse and pounding down the path away from her. Beatrice stared at him, eyes wide and body tingling in new and terrifying ways she didn't understand.

All she knew was that she liked the way she felt. And in the most secret places of her heart, mind and body, she couldn't wait to explore more sensuality with the Marquis of Highcroft.

And to appease her curiosity about the "proclivities" he had intimated he possessed. The ones that titillated as much as frightened her.

Chapter Five

Once the agreement had been struck, Beatrice was shocked by how quickly the marquis moved to fulfill his part of the arrangements. Within a day she had written a letter inviting her mother to join her sisters at Penelope's house party. Somehow Gareth managed to have it posted so it appeared to have come from her brother-in-law the Duke of Kilgrath's country home.

With perfect timing, Beatrice had revealed to her mother that *she* had been invited to join Amelia's family in the country. When faced with a choice between meddling in Beatrice's failed love life and hobnobbing with earls and dukes and people of import, her mother had been very clear.

Oh, of course when Dorthea appeared unannounced at her daughter's home, there would be much suspicion, but by then it would be too late. Her sisters, if they bothered to make search at all, would likely be unable to find her. After all, Beatrice had been careful not to share her plans with anyone, so there was no one to betray her confidence if her family investigated further.

And so Beatrice now found herself in a carriage with a very quiet female chaperone Gareth had sent along to fetch her. Whatever the servant thought of her, Beatrice did not know, for the girl kept to herself, hardly speaking during the entire half day's journey from London.

In some ways, the chaperone's silence frustrated Beatrice. At least if the other woman talked, Beatrice wouldn't find her mind slipping to the devil's bargain she had quite possibly made. And to the dangerous situation she was about to enter.

After all, as much as she tried to ignore and forget it, the fact was that Gareth Berenger was thought to have been involved in the death of his first wife. When Beatrice spoke to him, she found it hard to believe that to be true, but she didn't know his innocence for a fact. Once they were alone, he could do anything to her. And he had already intimated that his sexual desires were depraved.

As the carriage slowed she shivered, and it wasn't entirely with displeasure.

"They're opening the gates, miss," the servant said without looking up from her book. "We should be at the main house before a quarter of an hour has passed."

Beatrice glared at her companion. "So it turns out you *are* capable of speech, after all. What a relief."

The servant's gaze came up for a brief glance, but then she returned to her reading without reply. It took all the self-control Beatrice had not to throw something at her.

She shut her eyes for the remainder of the journey and found the carriage stopping what seemed like an interminable time later. The door opened and a hand reached in to help her out. When she took it and stepped down, she was surprised to find it was Gareth who greeted her, not a servant.

"H—hello," she stammered as she touched her feet to the drive and looked up at him. Up and up at him, actually. Had he always been so tall?

"Good afternoon, Beatrice," he said softly as he maneuvered her so the servants could begin unloading her things.

She hardly noticed as people shuffled back and forth around them. All she could think about was that Gareth was still holding her hand.

"Are you going to say something?" he asked with an eyebrow arched in obvious amusement.

Beatrice snatched her hand from his, blushing as she realized she had been staring up at him like some besotted schoolgirl.

"Could you have sent a duller servant to chaperone me?" she asked as she peeled off her gloves and strode into the house without waiting for his invitation. "She hardly spoke four words the entire journey. I was bored beyond belief."

"Perhaps you should have brought a book."

Beatrice jumped. Gareth was right at her elbow, though

she hadn't heard or felt his presence beside her. She turned on him.

"Perhaps. Now please have someone show me to my chamber, I am tired and I wish to refresh myself."

He stared at her and he laughed, low and dangerous. "No, no, no, Beatrice. This shall not do at all."

She stepped back, but he moved forward and crowded her against the wall.

"What do you mean?" she asked and found herself to be quite breathless.

"You and I made a bargain, my dear. You are mine for a fortnight. And if you think you shall spend it dictating to me, then you shall be very disappointed, indeed."

"What do you mean, I am *yours*?" Beatrice asked, her heart beginning to pound. "I never agreed to such a foolish thing."

"But you did, my dear." He braced one hand on each side of her head. She felt his warm breath on her skin and hated herself for liking it so much. "You see, you said you could stand my proclivities, whatever they may be. If that is true, then by the time this fortnight is over, you shall be bowing to my will whenever I demand it. You shall be my devoted sexual servant, Beatrice, and you will be thanking me for it."

Gareth had never used such blunt terms to describe what it was he longed for in bed. With the ladies he paid, there was no explanation necessary. Lightskirts had a much broader view of sex. Still, those encounters had never been very satisfying because there was no true surrender in them. Those women did what they did for blunt, not for the pure satisfaction of submitting.

So he had married, with the hopes that he could coax Laurel into surrender. When he had described his fantasies and desires to her, he had been gentle, for all the good it had done him in the end.

But with Beatrice, that would not do. To obtain her body, he needed to be perfectly clear about what he would do to her. And he reveled in how her eyes widened and her lower lip trembled even as she tried to glare at him with a mixture of disgust and disdain. She didn't quite achieve it. Behind her anxiety was definite interest and desire.

"I shall never be so foolish, I promise you," she spat back.

"Then I fear we won't match well at all, my dear," he said, calling her bluff with the one fear he actually knew she would admit to. After all, she had made this shocking bargain with him. Her straits were dire, indeed.

She flinched, just as he had known she would. For a long moment, she seemed to ponder what he said and then she nodded.

"Very well, Gareth," she said through clenched teeth. "You lead the way."

"Oh, I will," he all but purred before he took her hand and slipped it into the crook of his arm. She stiffened beneath his touch, her natural desire to resist, to argue bucking one last time. But when he maneuvered her toward the stairway, she didn't resist. While he wouldn't have described her as meek, when she followed him, she was definitely a kitten with her claws retracted.

He wondered how long that would last.

The question only lasted in his mind a few short moments for as he opened the door to his chamber and motioned her in, her brief acquiescence ended.

"Is this—" she broke off as she looked around the dark, very masculine room. He doubted she knew her blue eyes were so impossibly wide. "Is this *your* room?"

He nodded as he slipped the door shut behind him.

She shook her head when her gaze moved to the pile of trunks his servants had already efficiently deposited in the corner to be unpacked later.

"But those are *my* things!"

"Indeed, they are."

She turned on him, folding her arms below her breasts as she speared him with a very angry, very pointed glare.

"Where is my chamber?"

"You'll be sharing this one with me," he said softly. "I want access to you whenever I desire. However I desire."

"No." She shook her head. "Absolutely not. You promised me you would protect my reputation, you promised me—"

"Don't be an idiot, my dear," Gareth snapped, finally coming toward her. "Everyone on my staff is full aware that the only reason a lady would come without chaperone to stay here is to fuck in my bed."

She flinched at the blunt term, but did not look away. God, how he loved the fire in her eyes.

"There is no use simpering and pretending by providing you with a separate chamber that I will either invade every night or drag you from in your nightshift. You will stay with me, you will do as I please and my servants will politely look the other way and keep silent. Your reputation is something you have ruined in your own way. But there will be no further damage from this stay, I assure you."

Beatrice was silent for a long moment and Gareth could see that always-present war in her eyes. The one between her tart nature and what she thought she had to do in order to win his agreement to marry her. But her nature was strong and this time it won out.

He smiled as she stormed forward, one finger extended toward him like a tiny sword.

"How *dare* you talk to me about reputation? I am the only one risking anything for this devil's bargain, and what I have to win is very slim, indeed, considering what I will surrender before I am finished. Should I not have some say in what will happen to me? Some—"

He slipped a hand around her waist and dragged her against him. The action stopped her mouth and she simply stared up at him in a combination of fear and desire. The fact that the second emotion was there gave him great pleasure.

"I promise you, Beatrice, what you will receive will be pleasurable," he murmured.

She shivered as he brought his lips to her throat, but she still stammered, "I–I somehow doubt that. I have said I would do this for the end result, do not confuse yourself that I will take any pleasure from it."

"You are such a little liar," Gareth chuckled as he found the first button along the back of Beatrice's silken gown. He popped it free and she gasped.

"I am not," she whispered.

"Of course you are." He freed another button slowly, but kept his gaze focused firmly on her. "You can say you don't plan to enjoy anything I want to do with you, *to* you . . . but when I kissed you in Hyde Park, your reaction was explosive with a passion you have been taught to repress. Come, Miss Beatrice Albright, do not play games with me. There is some part of you that thrills at the idea of experiencing wicked, wanton pleasure. Some piece of you that aches when you imagine what I shall do with your body."

He freed three more buttons in rapid succession and her gown began to gape around the scooped neck, giving him a lovely tunnel view to the curve of her cleavage.

"Admit it," he whispered.

Beatrice shook her head. "I admit nothing."

He smiled and dipped his head down to glide his tongue between her breasts. She sucked in her breath and arched helplessly against him.

"Yes, you do," he murmured. "You admit everything with your body's reactions. You will tell me the same with your mouth later."

He tugged and her dress fell forward.

Beatrice felt the warm flush of blood to her cheeks and

hated the missish reaction. She didn't want to appear weak before this man, but that was exactly how she felt. Weak with the desire he could read plainly, but also weak with fear she hoped he would never sense.

This idea had been fine when it was only in theory, but now . . . now her gown was being glided down her hips, now Gareth was staring at her flesh openly, now she was really in this moment. And once they were finished, there would be no going back for her.

"You are beautiful," Gareth said softly as her dress hit the floor and left her only in a thin shift, stockings and slippers.

Even more heat flooded her face, but this time it was the heat of pleasure and she felt herself relax. No one had said she was beautiful in so long, she could scarce remember it.

"There is no need to fear," he said even softer as he enveloped her in the warm darkness of his embrace. She felt him gliding her backward ever so slowly, until her backside hit the edge of his bed. She started at the contact, but his strong arms wouldn't allow her to maneuver away.

"This first time, no games, no tests," he said, his tone strangely soothing in the otherwise silent room.

She could hardly breathe for a moment as the reality hit her once again. Only this time, with Gareth's arms firmly around her, with her breasts flat against his chest, her legs tangled with his, his bed at her back . . . somehow the reality was not chilling.

Shutting her eyes, she nodded. "Th—thank you," she whispered.

The statement sounded odd to her, for it was one she rarely said, but it fit here. After all, he could do anything, but he was promising her gentleness and care. The least she owed him was thanks as she endured what was to come.

"Look at me."

It was an order, which normally chafed Beatrice, but she found herself obeying. She let her eyes flutter open and watched as Gareth slowly divested himself of his jacket. He opened his cravat and then he tugged his shirt from his trouser waist. She held her breath as he opened it and pulled it over his head, leaving him naked from the waist up.

Good Lord, he was a sight. His olive skin looked warm as it stretched over an abundance of lean muscle. A light dusting of hair curled over that, trailing off into the waistband of the trousers he was now unbuttoning.

"You have never seen a man like this," he mused.

Somehow she tore her gaze from the shocking sight of the gaping fly of his pants and looked at him.

"No," she admitted.

"Not a servant? Not a relative? Not even a picture?" he asked.

She shook her head. "Nothing. Never."

He smiled as he pushed his trousers away and stood before her in full nudity. "And what do you think?"

She swallowed as she let her gaze move downward again. She had heard about a man's . . . instrument . . . his *cock*, she had heard her married sisters giggling about once. She had tried to picture it, but it had never been like *this* in her daydreams.

He was thick, the swollen thrust of him probably close to the width of her three fingers pressed together. As for length, she hadn't expected that, either.

"You are to fit that inside of me?" she asked, trying to picture such a thing. She might not have ever seen a man naked, but she had certainly touched herself. With one finger inside of her channel she felt full.

Before he answered, she watched as his cock actually changed.

"It is moving," she whispered.

"You *are* an innocent," he murmured, seemingly more to himself than to her. "As I become more excited by you, my cock fills and becomes harder. When it is fully erect, I will slide it inside of you. If I have done my job correctly, your body will be hot and slick and ready to stretch to receive me."

She looked up, his words giving her a shiver she could not suppress.

"Is it fully erect now?" she asked with another unwanted blush.

After a long moment of holding her gaze, he reached out and took her hand. He pulled her closer as he closed her fingers around him. She gasped at the silkiness of his skin in comparison to the hardness of the muscle beneath.

"Stroke me," he said, his voice strained.

Beatrice glanced up, her eyes wide. But she didn't pull back, despite the fact that he was ordering her around again. Instead, she glided her hand up and down his length, too mesmerized by the feel of him to stop herself from exploring her curiosity.

"Do you feel me getting harder with your touch?" he asked as he dropped his mouth to just below her ear.

She shivered as he stroked his tongue along the delicate skin there. "Yes," she managed to squeak out. "I feel it."

"I am almost ready to fill you," he groaned. "However, I doubt you are ready to receive me." With an unexpected shove, he toppled her across the bedsheets. "And so I have some work of my own to do."

Beatrice sat up on her elbows, half terrified of what he meant and half thrilled. She had never felt so shivery and achy, so nervous and excited all at once.

He leaned over her and she gasped as he grasped her ankle. His long, lean fingers curled around her and he lifted her foot up and glided her slipper off. He repeated the action on the opposite foot and tossed the shoes aside. He pushed her legs open just a fraction, which let him stand beside the bed between them. Beatrice gasped as warm air whispered over her naked skin, brushing under her chemise to her most private areas and intensifying the strange, throbbing ache there.

"A tease without even knowing it." He chuckled. She followed his line of sight and blushed as she realized he was looking to where her chemise had slipped between her spread thighs and partially covered her.

She couldn't think of a retort, she couldn't think of anything except for the feel of his fingers as he slid them up her legs. They tickled over her knees, they smoothed her thighs until he found the tops of her stockings. One by one, he rolled them away. His fingers glided over her bare, goose-pimpled flesh as he tugged them down and tossed them aside.

He joined her on the raised bed, crawling up on his knees and spreading her legs even farther with the width of his body.

She was torn by two reactions. One was to run away before it was too late to turn back. The other was to sit up and pull him down onto her flesh. To wrap his warmth around her, fill herself with it. She did neither—just lay there, helpless as she let his hands touch her again.

This time his palms settled on her bare thighs. She found her back arching as powerful pleasure moved through her at the shocking touch. The tingling between her legs grew stronger, and she felt the same wetness that gathered there when she touched herself rush to her body now.

His hands glided up until they reached the lower hem of her chemise. He met her eyes and slid it up, pushing the fabric over her hips and baring her from the waist down.

"Wait," she gasped, grasping his wrists and pushing gently as sensation and emotion overwhelmed her.

"Are you changing your mind?" he murmured as he settled down lower. His head hovered over her stomach, his eyes locked with hers, his body comfortable between her thighs.

She hesitated. Was she?

"I—I don't know," she finally admitted. "This is all so strange."

"Let go," he whispered and then his head dipped down. "Just let go, Beatrice."

Before she could think, let alone respond, his hands moved to her inner thighs, pushing her wide and spreading the outer lips of her most private places open. She was exposed as his head dipped there and she couldn't help but gasp out a cry when his lips touched there.

"What?" she cried out, her elbows giving out as she fell back against the mattress. "Gareth?"

He didn't answer, just glided his tongue out and pressed it to her hot, wet flesh. He simply lapped at her entrance at first, reminding her of the second time he kissed her in the park. He had breached her lips with such unexpected delicacy and gentleness. Now he did the same, but with her lower lips. And just as she had in the park, she felt herself surrendering to the sensation.

When she relaxed, it seemed to be a cue to him, for the lapping strokes of his tongue intensified. He flattened his tongue to her flesh, the pressure of his mouth growing more insistent and focused, like he was determined to clean away every drop of her juices and replace them with his own.

And it was magnificent. If her sheath had fluttered and ached before, now he awakened her nerves, her flesh all the more. Nothing she had ever done alone in the quiet of her bed could compare to this touch. This utterly wicked tasting.

His fingers joined in, spreading her open, tracing her entrance with seductive slowness. And then finally, with a flick of his wrist he found that place she always rubbed, that little hard, smooth pearl of her pleasure that was hidden within her folds. While his tongue breached and pleasured her channel, he rubbed that hidden pearl with his finger and thumb in a way more intense than anything she had done. Her hips began to buck in time to his pleasuring, moans escaped her lips and finally, with a burst of wetness and trembling, pleasure overwhelmed her and she lost all control.

By the time the overpowering sensations subsided, Beatrice couldn't have said if moments or hours had passed. All she could do was lie back, panting, feeling her heart throb and her body twitch out the last few grasps at the pleasure she had experienced. She looked down the stretch of her body to see Gareth licking his lips as he moved up toward her.

He kissed her as he settled over her and she tasted an earthly, salty flavor on his lips. With a start, she realized it was herself she was tasting. Her mind told her to turn her head, but her body arched up instead, molding to Gareth's hard angles.

"Now you're ready. And I am most definitely ready," he said when he broke from her mouth. His eyes sparkled with intent and desire as he stared down at her.

She tensed when he positioned his hips and she felt the nudging of his cock against her entrance. Reality pierced her fog and she looked at him with what she knew was fear and hesitation. He held her gaze for a moment before he dropped his lips to hers and slid forward.

Beatrice stiffened at the breach, but instead of fully seating himself inside of her, Gareth hesitated. The moment of respite allowed her to truly experience the moment. She felt full, far fuller than when she touched herself, but it was not unpleasant as she had feared when she first looked upon his member. It was simply foreign and strange, but also thrilling.

She shifted below him, squeezing her internal muscles experimentally and reveling in the tingle of pleasure that echoed from that action. Above her Gareth closed his eyes with a harsh groan and she stared at him. Had *she* done that?

"You are testing my patience," he murmured and slid forward another inch. "In the very best way possible."

"Why be patient?" she panted as she strained up around him.

"Because I want this to be pleasurable for you," he gasped as he moved forward again. "And if I rush it will be less than so."

Beatrice met his gaze again, taken aback by how intimate it felt to be so close to someone else. Being joined as they were was frightening because she felt so revealed, so dangerously vulnerable . . . and yet, for the first time in her life, she was willing to be so because the reward for her vulnerability was so sweet.

His mouth dropped down, covering hers. She sank into the kiss, tightening her arms around the broad expanse of his muscled back. Her remaining anxiety faded and she simply *felt*, just as he had asked her to when they began.

Gareth took that moment to drive the last few inches home into her body. She stiffened as he breached her maidenhead, the pain of the final joining a stark reminder that pierced her haze.

He looked down at her and Beatrice was surprised to see the empathy and guilt that darkened his gaze.

"It will never be like that again," he reassured her softly.

She nodded, though she wasn't totally certain she could trust any promise he made. Still, her sisters did not seem to mind what they shared with their husbands, so that gave credence to his pledge.

"And now I want to erase this pain," he whispered.

His mouth returned to hers in a deep kiss that made her stomach clench and her blood boil. Despite the remaining pain, she shivered at his touch. At the feel of him stretching her untried body. Then he moved and she forgot everything but the new sensations that rushed through her in a powerful burst.

He arched his hips against her, driving himself deep within her womb and rubbing her pelvis in such a way that the pleasure he had evoked earlier with his tongue was intensified to new heights. She arched into each driving motion, lifting herself to meet him, digging her nails into his bare flesh as she cried out in pleasure over and over.

He had promised he would make her forget the pain of their joining, and he was fulfilling his word with great skill. All she could feel now, could see now, could experience now, was him. In that moment, the pleasure exploded.

She slammed her hips against his from below as she wailed out a great sound of pleasure and completion. Then she collapsed back on the bed, gasping for air as she watched him withdraw and spend against the bedsheets.

Shutting her eyes, Beatrice heaved out a great sigh. There. It was done. And there was no going back, not until she had this man's ring on her finger.

Chapter Six

Gareth found himself staring at Beatrice as she lay, a bare arm flopped over her eyes, her breasts rising and falling as she panted out breath. Her skin sparkled with sweat, made pink from his touch and from the flush of orgasm.

He hadn't expected their first joining to be so powerful. Or to find her such an enthusiastic and exciting partner. After all, her reputation was an icy one and she was a virgin, not experienced in matters of the flesh. And yet she had brought him great pleasure and reinforced his thought that she could be a very good partner to him.

If only she passed his tests.

As if she sensed him staring, Beatrice moved her arm away from her face and looked up at him. To his surprise, he could not read her expression.

"You are not the monster you pretended to be," she finally said as she pushed up on her elbows.

He arched a brow at her unexpected statement. "What do you mean?"

"You made me think you would be utterly depraved, that you would demand unconscionable things from me that I might not be able to accept. And yet, what happened between us did not seem to be so . . ." She hesitated. "Bad."

He almost laughed. Was she trying to be insulting or could she simply not help herself? He rolled on his side to face her, watching how her nipples tightened when he came nearer, how her eyes glazed. She wanted him, and he liked that he could coax such a response from a woman known more for her sharpness than her passion.

"I think you may not understand," he said softly as he reached out to trace her arm with a fingertip. Her pale skin flushed at even this light touch. "Today I took your virginity. That is an immense responsibility and I took it seriously. I wasn't about to introduce you to all my 'depravities,' as you put it, when you were untried and uncertain. And what we did together *did* give me great pleasure."

He could have sworn that her eyes lit up with surprised delight before she turned her face.

"But . . ." she supplied.

He shrugged. "I wouldn't be kept satisfied for long by the simplicity of what we just shared. I need more."

She sat up now and grabbed for the coverlet to wrap around her body. He recognized the action was a way to shield herself and for now he allowed it. Soon enough he would peel away all her protection, break her shell.

"But you have never fully explained to me what *more* means, Gareth. What is it that you want that is so fearful to other women?"

He cocked his head. He supposed she did deserve to know.

"It is not enough for me to claim your body, Beatrice," he said softly. "When you are in my bed, I need to own you. To feel you bend to my will. To see you accept me as your master."

She was silent for a long while, simply staring at him with eyes wide. "You want a slave."

"In bed, yes," he admitted without a hint of shame. He felt none.

She shook her head as she threw the covers back and scrambled from the bed.

"You tricked me!" she cried as she grabbed for her discarded chemise and threw it over her head.

He watched without moving. "And how did I do that?"

"You should have told me you wanted a slave, you should have told me before you took my virtue." She looked around as she covered her mouth. "Good Lord, I can't do that. I can't surrender everything to you."

"Why not?"

He pushed off the bed and she took a long step away from him as he grabbed for a robe that was draped across the foot of the bed.

She blinked. "You have seen my nature, you have heard

what others say. I—I am not built for such a thing. To give a man everything, especially one whom I know so little about . . . that is asking too much."

"But you already did that." He smiled. "You could have asked me at any time about what I expected from you, what my proclivities were. Instead you came here and blindly offered yourself to me."

She shook her head. "Because I had no choice!"

"No." Gareth smiled. "You *always* had a choice, but some part of you wanted to be under my control. Part of you was titillated at not knowing what I would do once I had you under my power."

"That isn't true," she whispered, but despite the strength of her denial, he saw the truth glittering in her eyes, even if she couldn't yet accept it.

"Yes, it is." He reached out and covered her shoulder with his hand. She blinked, but didn't move away. He could have crowed with delight. "Don't you see? All this is the first step, Beatrice. You are already on the road to total and utter surrender. And your sharp nature is part of why I desired you so deeply. You are like a wild filly that needs to be broken."

"You are the most insulting man. I'm not a *horse!*" she snapped and turned away.

He slipped up behind her. She was trembling and the slight movement ricocheted through him. This time, he didn't touch her, but leaned in close to her ear.

"No, you most certainly are not. But think of how much pleasure I gave you today."

She drew in a breath to refute what he already knew but he reached around and covered her lips gently with his fingers.

"Don't deny it, I felt and saw your pleasure very clearly. Think of it, Beatrice. And think of what I could do to you, *for* you, if you were mine in every way."

There was a moment where he felt her considering this, but she wouldn't allow herself to yield. She spun on him.

"No!"

He folded his arms. This was all part of the dance, and in the end, it would be he who led her, or else they could never be truly happy together.

"If you cannot even try, then you should probably go now," he said softly, knowing exactly what her reaction would be. "I'll fulfill my end of our bargain and provide you with the settlement we arranged. You may return to London at any time; you are not a hostage here." He hesitated. "Return to your *mother*."

That made her flinch, and he almost felt sorry for her as she paced away from him to look out the window over his gardens. Although she tried desperately not to show it, Gareth sensed the vulnerability and desperation in Beatrice that she fought so hard to hide beneath her sharp exterior. She knew exactly what would occur if she gave up on their arrangement now.

And he was willing to wager that she wasn't prepared to let that happen.

She turned on him slowly. "Will you hurt me? Beat me?"

He shook his head just as slowly. "Of course not. Dominance does not have to involve pain. And I would never raise a hand to a woman."

She tilted her head slightly and looked at him with an appraising stare. He almost flinched away from it, for he knew she was thinking of his late wife. Of the rumors that he had, indeed, hurt a woman.

"I cannot promise I'll surrender," she said. "It isn't in my nature."

"That is half the pleasure, Beatrice," he said, unable to keep a feral smile from his lips. "You are a challenge."

He stepped toward her and she lurched back. His smile faded. Clearly, he had not yet fully convinced her that he would not hurt her physically. He sighed as he gathered his clothing from the floor.

"You are likely sore at present. I have already made arrangements for you to have a warm bath. You may take your time and join me for supper at seven."

Beatrice stared at him. "You—you are finished with me?"

He nodded. "For now."

"But—" She hesitated. "But why?"

A shrug was his answer as he pulled his trousers over his hips. "I have a fortnight for my pleasure." He smiled at her again. "Why rush? I will see you tonight."

Then he turned and left her to think about what had occurred. And, he hoped, to fantasize about what was to come.

Beatrice would not have admitted it out loud, but the bath was quite restorative, not just to her sore body, but to her racing mind. As she sank down deeper beneath the warm embrace of the water, her troubles and fears drained away, leaving her with only memories of the pleasures she had experienced that day.

She had often imagined what making love to a man would be like. Even as it became clearer and clearer that her chances at marriage were fading, she had still dreamed of passion and, even in her silliest moments, love. She had even touched herself, though she had never felt anything like the explosive, blinding release he had given her today.

No, nothing she had dreamed or done came close to sharing her body with Gareth. His hands, his mouth, his cock . . . they had brought her such sensations she had never imagined. She had never felt closer to another person in her life.

And yet he wanted *more*. He wanted surrender, obedience. He wanted to be her master.

The very thought terrified her, but lurking behind the terror was something else: excitement. She could try to deny the thrill all she wanted, but the idea of turning herself over to Gareth completely did make her insides tingle and her hands shake.

She frowned. Less than an hour had passed since Gareth touched her and yet she ached for more pleasure. More than ached—she was obsessed. All she could think about was her throbbing sheath, the tingling pearl hidden within her folds.

On the other side of the screen that surrounded the tub, she could hear a servant bustling about and tidying up as she put Beatrice's things away. Did she dare bring herself plea-sure when the young woman could hear or see?

Her body throbbed and Beatrice slipped her hand below the water's surface to cover the mound between her legs. The touch did not ease her ache, but intensified it. She increased the pressure against her folds and bit back a sigh of pleasure at the feel. Just a few moments couldn't hurt. Not if she was quiet.

She bent her fingers and the tips slid between the folds until she caressed the slick wetness of her slit. The flesh was tender from Gareth's invasion, but that only served to make her more sensitive. Even just this slight touch made her hips buck and a gasp escape her lips. Never had her own fingers brought her such stimulation. It was intense. Addictive.

"Are you quite well, miss?" came the servant's voice from around the screen. "May I bring you something?"

Beatrice closed her eyes and tried to measure her breathing before she answered. "N–no. I'm fine. Just continue in your duties."

She heard the girl moving about again and shivered. There was something so wicked about doing this with another person in the room. Someone who had no idea about how she was touching herself. She let her fingers slide deeper into her sheath and began to slowly work them in and out of her body, mimicking what Gareth had done to her earlier.

To her shock, the tingles of pleasure began to rise, giving her a faint taste of the explosion of release she was work-ing toward. Could she truly give herself that? She certainly

craved that feeling with an intensity that was almost frightening, for it was out of control, guiding her emotions and
actions more than her logic was.

She ground down over herself, driving her fingers deeply
inside of herself, then she found the pearl of her pleasure with
her thumb and flicked over it. Unexpectedly, release overtook
her, powerful and intense as her hips bucked wildly, making
water slosh over the tub's edge to *thwack* onto the floor. She
didn't care. She rode out the pleasure, breathing heavily,
trying to keep herself from a scream of pleasure. Finally she
covered her mouth with her free hand, biting into the flesh to
remain silent.

The tremors finally subsided, leaving her to collapse back
against the tub in sated shock. She lay there for a long moment
and then her eyes came open and she stared above her. The
girl on the other side of the screen continued her bustling.
Had she heard? If so, what did she think?

Beatrice smiled. Did it matter? As Gareth had said earlier,
his servants had to be aware of why she was here. She was
staying in their master's room. If the girl thought she was
a wanton, then let her. Perhaps Beatrice was becoming one,
after all.

She shivered when the word *master* entered her mind.
Gareth would be a very different kind of master to her if she
decided to allow him his fantasy. But total surrender . . . that
was terrifying. She didn't want to entirely depend upon another person for anything, even her pleasure. There was too
much risk involved in being so vulnerable.

But she was stuck, wasn't she? Her maidenhead was gone, the value of it to another man dashed away. That meant Gareth was truly her best choice. If she could only survive . . . convince him that she was completely and utterly his, he would marry her and set her free from her mother. Once that was done, she could go away to London or another of his estates. In reality, she only had to make him *think* he had won her soul.

She could do that, couldn't she? Play along with his game until she got what she wanted?

"Are you ready to come out now, miss?" the girl's voice came from the other side of the barrier.

Beatrice thought about the question. Was she ready? Ready for Gareth, ready for his games? If she played some of her own . . . perhaps she was.

"Yes," she said, rising up so she would be ready when the girl brought the warm towel around to her. "I'm ready for anything."

When Beatrice entered the dining hall that evening, Gareth sensed a change in her from the vulnerable, uncertain girl he had left in his bed. When she entered the room, her shoulders were thrust back, making the rose pink silk of her gown strain against the curve of her breasts. She walked with purpose as she moved into the room and allowed a servant to seat her at his right hand. And when she looked at him, it was directly in his eye.

"Good evening, Beatrice," he said with a smile as he snapped his napkin across his lap.

She nodded before she took a bracing sip of red wine. He watched her throat work as she swallowed and thought of all the things he wanted to teach her to do with that pretty, full mouth.

"I can see you have been thinking about our talk earlier," he said.

She nodded. "I have."

"And have you come to a decision? Should I send for the carriage to take you home . . . or should I ready myself for the next fortnight with you?"

Her gaze came to his and held, even and so beautifully blue. At first glance all her stare held was chilly detachment, but Gareth wanted to delve deeper. He had seen her vulnerability before. He knew it was under there, hiding because she feared showing it.

"I can't leave, can I?" she finally said softly.

"Of course you can," he drawled.

She pursed her lips in frustration. "You know I cannot return to London and the lack of prospects and future I have there. So, I will stay and make an attempt to please you."

He smiled. She made it sound like such a chore. "You must have thought very heavily about this while you readied yourself for supper after I left you."

She nodded as a servant placed the first course before them. "I did. It hardly left my mind."

"Even while you brought yourself to pleasure in the bath?" he asked mildly.

Beatrice had taken a spoonful of soup before he spoke and her eyes widened as she began to cough. He waited for her to regain her composure.

"Wha—what are you talking about?" she asked when she had wiped her mouth.

"My dear, my servants will never breathe a word about you to anyone outside the house, but they are loyal to me." Gareth leaned closer, grabbed the edge of Beatrice's chair and dragged it toward him. "You can pretend you are resigned to what I've offered you, but in truth it excites you. Enough that you pleasured yourself with a servant in the room."

She turned her face, her cheeks filled with hot color, but Gareth sensed her titillation at the idea that the maid knew what she had done. That a stranger had reported her erotic actions to Gareth. He leaned forward and pressed his mouth to her throat.

Beatrice moaned and tilted her neck back for greater access, but then she seemed to come to her senses and shook her head. "No, here? At the table?"

"Anywhere I want you, Beatrice," he answered before he pushed her chair back into its original position. "Any *time* I want you."

She shivered as she stared at him, slightly less pulled together than she had been when she entered the dining room. He could actually feel her physical barriers coming down. Already she was more open to what he wanted than Laurel ever had been.

But a physical surrender wasn't enough. He didn't want pretend obedience and submission. He wanted her to lay out her entire being to his care. Inside and out.

He took a sip of wine. "I want something right now."

She nodded, her brow arching as she tried to regain some of her distance. "I can see that."

She stared pointedly at his crotch and Gareth glanced down at his ballooning erection with a dismissive shrug.

"That isn't what I want . . . yet." He slid his chair forward and leaned closer. "I want to know more about you. There is little information to be found beyond a pedigree of your family and the rumors spread about your poor attitude."

Her hands clenched against the table and her gaze darted away. "What else matters but pedigree and rumor, my lord? Those things make the world go around."

Gareth leaned back and folded his arms. The porcupine element of her personality was back. Her tone was sharp, her body language said to stay far away. Any softness he had seen earlier in his bed was gone.

"Pedigree and rumor have gotten us here, but if we are to marry at some point, I think a bit more will be required, pet." He tilted his head. "Tell me about your father. He died some years back, did he not?"

The color drained from Beatrice's face and she simply *stared* at him for a long, charged moment. Then she shook her head.

"It hardly matters now, does it? He is dead. I do not wish to speak of him."

Gareth's eyebrows went up at the stony and flat expression on her face. She was a wall now, one there would be no breaching. Yet.

"Very well," he said, ready to give her a small bit of ground at the beginning. "Then your mother. You two are obviously close in some ways, and yet you long to escape her. What can you tell me about her?"

"She is what you see. What else is there to say?" Beatrice snapped, and drank another long sip of wine.

"Then what about your sisters?" he asked, frustration mounting in him at her utter stonewalling. "I would very much doubt any of them can be defined only by what you see. I have heard whispers about both Lady Rothschild and the Duchess of Kilgrath and how they managed to marry the men in their lives."

"If you have heard whispers, then why ask me?" She sniffed. "You already seem to know all. Why would I know more?"

"Because they are your blood," he pressed.

She shrugged as if she couldn't care less. "Just because they are my blood, it does not necessarily follow that I know anything about them of interest, or that they know anything about me."

Gareth stared. Whatever she felt about her family, it was something so powerful that she actually seemed to *fear* sharing any part of it with him. That kind of barrier was what he would have to destroy if he was to dominate her entirely.

She had to trust him or else he would never truly have her full submission and surrender.

When a few silent moments had passed, Gareth said, "I find it interesting that you will share your body with me, that you will even agree to submit to my other demands . . . and yet you are so reticent to share even the barest hint of your past. You won't allow even a glimpse of your inner thoughts."

Beatrice turned her face so that Gareth could only see her in profile, but by the thin line of her mouth and the worry around her eyes, he could see the internal battle she was waging.

Finally she tapped her fingernails nervously against the edge of the plate beneath her soup bowl.

"I have found in my life that the most damage, the most hurt can be done by people who know my past . . . or my thoughts. Why should I give anyone a weapon like that to use against me?" Her gaze moved to him. "Especially you, whom I do not know beyond one encounter in bed. Why should I trust you?"

He drew back, surprised that she would admit these thoughts. Yes, these were all first steps. Still, he had to be careful in his response.

"What I want to do, to share with you, will require some trust, Beatrice."

She shrugged. "Well, perhaps I will be able to grant you that, and perhaps I will not. Time will tell, won't it?"

Gareth watched her for a long moment. Beatrice was blunt, she had been called a bitch for her coldness, but he understood that on so many levels. Her attitude was her shield, her protection. Unfortunately, she had been so long in the habit of protecting herself that he was not certain if he could ever force her to release that habit. But the longer he spent around her, the more interested he became in breaking down her barriers. In overcoming her obstacles.

In making her his in every way possible.

"Yes," he said as he raised his glass in salute to her. "Only time will tell."

Chapter Seven

When Beatrice had refused to share anything of her personal past with Gareth at dinner, somehow she had expected an inquisition for the rest of the evening . . . and perhaps even a trip home when she would not capitulate to his personal probing. She didn't want that, but what he asked her to share was too much for her.

However, the rest of the dinner passed in surprisingly companionable conversation. Gareth backed away completely from the personal topics she loathed, instead asking her about her pursuits and telling her about his own. It had been so long since she had shared in such civil discourse that she hardly knew how to respond.

But now they were walking together up the long hallway toward the staircase. Gareth didn't touch her, he wasn't even holding her elbow, and yet Beatrice felt his presence through every part of her. Simply standing near him made her feel like he was invading her space, filling her pores, touching her in ways that were wholly inappropriate.

Truth be told, she rather liked the feeling.

"I never got a chance to show you my home," Gareth said as he motioned up the stairs. "Would you like the tour?"

She nodded. "We won't start in the main area of the house, though?"

He shook his head. "My main house is really no different from anyone else's in Society. I have a magnificent ballroom that I never use, several boring parlors, a cluttered office, a billiard room, a music room . . . If you've seen one of those kinds of chambers, you've seen them all, just in different colors and with varying quality of furniture."

"I suppose so," Beatrice said slowly as she moved up the stairway behind Gareth. "Then why bother with the pretense of a tour at all?"

He smiled over his shoulder at her and Beatrice was put fully to mind of a cat with his prey. He was toying with her and it took every bit of her self-control not to lash out at him because of it. She didn't like being his game.

Or at least, she *thought* she didn't. Sometimes she wasn't sure. Being with him was rather like riding in an out-of-control phaeton. She feared and anticipated the next turn with equal measure.

"Because, my dear, there are places in this house that are

entirely out of the ordinary." He stopped before a door and pulled out a small golden key from his inside coat pocket. "Like this one."

Unlocking the door, he motioned her inside.

The chamber was dark, except for a low fire that hardly illuminated anything. It took a moment for her eyes to adjust, after the brightly lit hallway. She felt Gareth move and then a few lamps blazed forth and the fire raised.

Blinking, Beatrice looked around her. Part of the reason she'd had trouble seeing was that the room was decorated in black. Black curtains, black coverings on what little furniture surrounded her, even a black rug covered the polished wooden floors.

It was a devil's room with the devil's accoutrements. A long, wide table sat in the middle of the room, covered in soft, supple leather that put Beatrice to mind of a fine saddle. Attached to the leather were what looked to be matching restraints, some at one end, some at the other and some in the middle of the area, though these looked like they could be tucked away.

Along one wall hung a small collection of riding crops. When Beatrice saw those, she staggered back.

"What the hell is this?"

"A room for my pleasure," Gareth said mildly, as if he had shown her nothing more shocking than the boring billiard room he had described earlier. "And I hope it will become a room for yours, as well."

"These are *whips*, Gareth," Beatrice said, motioning wildly at the wall. "You told me you would never raise a hand to a woman."

Against her will, her mind spun wildly to the rumors surrounding him. The death of his wife, the idea that he could have been responsible. Had he beaten his wife with those crops on the wall? Terror filled Beatrice for just a moment before she stuffed it away.

"To be fair, I wouldn't be raising a *hand* to you," he said with a chuckle in his voice that grated along her spine. She hated that he was mocking her fear.

"You are not amusing, sir," she whispered, staying back from him.

He frowned and grew serious. "My dear, some people find that just a touch of pain greatly enhances the pleasure of sex. The barrier between the two is quite thin, you see."

Beatrice hesitated. When he said those words, she couldn't help but think of earlier when she had found release in his bed. The pleasure had been so intense that it *had* bordered on pain in some way. And later, in the tub, her sensitive, sore sheath had only magnified her own touch.

"But I would never force you to do such a thing. I do not require pain for my pleasure," he said, interrupting her shocking thoughts. "Though I certainly wouldn't mind trying if you decided you were interested."

Beatrice shivered, though she wasn't certain if the motion was caused by fear or disgust or titillation—perhaps it was a combination of all three.

"And what of the table?" she asked, her voice still hatefully shaky.

"I might want total control over you," he explained with another of his nonchalant shrugs. "Tying you down into whatever position I desire gives me that. The same is true for the restraints on the wall."

She followed the motion of his hand and gasped. She had been so shocked by the hanging selection of crops that she hadn't noticed the fur-lined restraints on the wall. Could a man truly take a woman like that?

A part of her wanted to find out.

"The idea of surrendering control truly frightens you," he said softly.

Beatrice jerked her gaze to his. Telling him about her fear was almost more frightening than physically surrendering to him in the ways he had described.

"Don't be ridiculous. I'm not frightened," she lied. "Only shocked, as any lady in my position would be."

"Hmm," he said.

It was obvious he didn't believe her. He stared for a moment before he crossed over to her. His hands came around her waist with more gentleness than she had expected and he molded her body to his own. She couldn't help it. She leaned into him, reveling in his scent and feel.

"Do you want me?" he asked. "Tell me you do."

She started. This order, it seemed different from the ones he had given her before. There was more urgency to it. This was the beginning of the surrender he had described.

Now she had to choose. Would she give him what he desired or say no?

"I do want you," she heard herself say, even before she had actually made the decision to do so.

"You want my body inside of yours," he clarified. "You wish to give yourself to me."

She nodded.

"No. Say it, Beatrice," his tone was sharp. "Say it out loud."

Again, she hesitated, loathe to lay so much of herself out for his inspection. But she had agreed to this, so she found herself whispering, "I want you to bury yourself in me."

His eyes closed and a low, animal moan rumbled from deep inside him. "Very nice."

She tilted her mouth up for his kiss, but he shook his head. Apparently his torture was not over.

"Now *ask* me," he said, his voice low and rough. "And say please."

Beatrice stiffened out of instinct, but his arms, which had been gentle at first, closed tighter around her. She looked up to find him staring back at her, waiting. If she refused, he would let her go. But she would get nothing.

And her body throbbed. It ached to be touched. What she had done for herself earlier in the day would not be enough, of that she was certain. She needed this man. Actually *needed* him, a troubling fact she refused to consider in that moment.

"Please take me," she whispered, her tone just barely audible.

He smiled. "That will do for now."

His mouth came down and crushed against hers with hungry, passionate pressure. She lifted up on her tiptoes to meet him, to get closer, to feel more, feel it faster. He lifted her up effortlessly and she found herself wrapping her legs around his back and clinging tightly.

Gareth reeled from Beatrice's passionate response. In truth, he had not expected such renewed ardor so quickly. He had been certain that she would hesitate. After all, she had been through a great deal that day, from the travel to the loss of her virtue, to the realization of exactly what he would take from her if she acquiesced.

In truth, he had intended only to show her this room tonight and then leave her to think about what would happen between them.

But now her dress was bunched between them, her legs were locked around his back, her mouth was hungry on his own . . . and his cock didn't give a damn how much she had been through. He wanted to fuck her. He wanted to do it here in this playroom. He wanted it now.

Without breaking the harsh contact of their lips, Gareth carried her over to the leather table in the middle of the room. He laid her back against the supple surface and covered her body with the curve of his own.

She arched into him with a low, needy moan and a shiver of pleasure worked its way through him. God, but she was responsive. And perfectly molded for the life he wished to introduce her to. Her resistance would only make the surrender later all the more pleasurable.

He pulled back and looked down at her, spread across the table, her hair beginning to come down from the pretty style she had worn at supper. Her gown was still tangled up around her thighs, the silky fabric wrinkled.

He smiled at her, and to his surprise, she returned the expression with a wicked one of her own. The spark between them was almost too much. With shaking fingers, he grasped the pretty dark pink ribbon that tied beneath her perfect breasts and tugged. The bow opened, revealing a line of flower-shaped buttons beneath. He made quick work of those, too, and pushed the gap in the cloth open wide.

His mouth came down as he shoved at the dress, moving it and the chemise beneath down over her arms and to her waist. Her breasts were pale in the glowing light of the chamber, their nipples a dark, dusky pink that almost matched her gown. Already they were hard, thrusting up toward him and begging to be sucked and touched.

He didn't resist, but dipped his head and sucked one into the cavern of his mouth. Beatrice's head thrashed against the table and her fingers curved against the smooth surface as if she were grasping for purchase on the leather. He sucked harder and she gasped.

He lifted his head. "You see what just a touch of pain can do, Beatrice?"

Her eyes narrowed and he watched as her gaze flitted toward the riding crops on the wall beside them. Then she returned her eyes to him.

"Do it again," she whispered.

He smiled. "No, no. *Ask* me."

Her lips thinned, but he didn't move.

"Please, do it again," she finally murmured.

"Do what?" he asked, determined to set her on the path he wanted.

She glared. "Please suck my nipples, Gareth."

His mouth came back to cover her flesh, only instead of sucking he gently scraped his teeth across the sensitive nub of flesh. Beatrice yelped, her back arching into him at the sensation.

He slipped his hands beneath her and pulled, curving her back so that her breasts were offered to him perfectly, then he attended to his business with more purpose than before. Back and forth he moved between them, suckling one nipple until it was red with pleasure, then abandoning it for the other. Then, with purposeful slowness, he began to languidly lick the valley between her breasts.

She was crying out by the time he stopped, her body shaking. He scented her desire on the air, and knew instinctively that if he put his hands between her thighs, if he touched her clit, she would come with explosive power.

But this was the beginning of her surrender, and if he gave her such pleasure without demanding something in return, she wouldn't fully understand or respect what he desired. So as tempting as her pleasure was, he did not touch her, but pulled her back to her feet.

She was panting, swaying as she stared at him. He remained silent as he watched her struggle with these new feelings of wanton desire, but did nothing. Finally she let out a harrumph of frustration.

"What do you want?" she asked, her sharp tone back. "Tell me."

"Good girl," he purred as he grasped the edging of her gown and pulled it free from her body to pool at her feet. "Now you are starting to understand."

She kicked her slippers away as she stared up at him. "Then tell me."

"Do you recall when I pleasured you with my tongue?"

Her blush answered as much as her quick nod. His cock throbbed at both, and at the memory of her earthy flavor, her powerful orgasm.

"I want to feel that mouth of yours around me," he said, unfastening his trousers and letting them drop away. "I want you to pleasure me."

As Beatrice stared down at Gareth's fully aroused cock, she couldn't help but shiver. She had her doubts that she could fit him between her lips, but once she did . . . what did she do then? It wasn't as if people explained these things to ladies of her station.

"There will be no pleasure for you, my dear, unless you try," he said softly.

She glared at him. Whether she would ever admit it to him or not, he held all the power here. Why *wouldn't* he use it? He had stated that the power was what he desired.

And worse, the subtle strength of his— Was it a threat?

Well, whatever it was, it made her tingle and want him even more.

"How?" she asked through clenched teeth. "Teach me."

He cocked his head, almost surprised at her quick acquiescence. "Get on your knees."

Hesitation filled her again. On her knees before this man? Practically worshipping him? But then again, the idea of giving him pleasure was such a powerful one. Wouldn't she have the upper hand if she did this right? For once, wouldn't he be a slave to her?

She slithered downward, kneeling on her discarded gown. Her face was even with the male thrust of him and she looked at it. The first time she looked upon him, she hadn't noticed all the detail of the mushroom head, the fine veins that lined it, the teardrop of his essence that leaked from the tip. Without thinking, she reached out and touched him, gripping him as he had instructed her to do earlier and stroking him from base to tip.

He moaned when she did so, bracing himself on the table where he had tortured her with his mouth just a few moments earlier.

Beatrice was uncertain, but to her surprise instinct began to kick in. Some sort of primal connection that came from hundreds of generations of women who had pleasured hundreds of generations of men. So when she leaned forward and touched just the pointed tip of her tongue to his cock, it did not feel as foreign or strange as she had thought.

In fact, it felt good. Right. She inched forward, grasping the base of his cock as she repeated the action, tonguing the tiny slit there as he had licked her earlier.

"Great God," he muttered from above her and his fingers laced into her hair.

"Is this right?" she asked, looking up at him in question. "This is how you taste me."

He gripped his fists at his sides as he slowly nodded. His voice was strained when he said, "I like when you do that, but I want more. More of your mouth, more of your tongue. I want to be inside your body, one way or another."

She thought about the actions he had taken when he took her body earlier in the day. If he wanted her to mimic those movements, then what she was doing wasn't quite right. She had been licking the opening, but now she understood. Her mouth was to be like her sheath, he wanted her to wrap herself around him like she had with her body when he made love to her.

Still uncertain, she drew him between her lips. He had an earthly flavor, not at all unpleasant and she rubbed her tongue on the underside of his member gently.

It must have been the right thing to do, for his hips lifted, pushing another few inches into her mouth and he let out a curse.

"Yes," he cried out. "Now move around me."

Slowly, she lowered her lips, taking more of his hardness into her mouth. When he hit her throat, she nearly gagged, but paused, relaxing her muscles as she struggled to take more of him, all of him.

She mimicked his thrusts from earlier in the day. Back and forth, a slow taking that drove him deep and then eased him almost out of her mouth entirely.

After a short time, she found a rhythm that was comfortable. She realized she liked the taste of him, she liked the feel of the head of his cock bumping the back of her throat. She most definitely liked his strangled moans as she pleasured him. Those little needy sounds made her body tingle and her most private, feminine parts ache to be touched.

His fingers unclenched at his sides and then she felt them in her hair, pushing her locks away so he could look down at her face.

She took him deeper and this time felt no discomfort. As she pulled away, she licked gently, tasting him, stimulating him and loving how he sucked in a harsh breath of pleasure and desire.

"Faster," he groaned, his fingers tangling against her scalp. She relaxed as he began to push, showing her how deeply he liked to be taken, how quickly.

It was amazing how easily she lost herself in an act she had never once considered or even pictured. If someone had told her a month ago that she would be taking a man's erect penis between her lips, she might have slapped them, but now . . . now she reveled in that act. Reveled in Gareth's passionate responses.

She kept one hand firmly wrapped around his cock, but with the other she snaked down her naked body and slipped her fingers between her legs. She found her mound and burrowed inside, teasing the pearl of her pleasure with rapid, forceful movements.

"Shit," Gareth groaned from above her.

Then suddenly she was being yanked away from him, dragged up his body. He pressed her back against the edge of the table and drove his tongue into her mouth, kissing her with purposeful thrusts as he rubbed his pelvis against hers.

She began to open her legs, to invite him to take what he had so aroused, but before she could settle back, she found herself being spun until her back was to him. He arched up, his cock briefly breaching the soft globes of her backside and pressing against the forbidden entrance there. But then he adjusted and she felt his cock at her slit again.

He bent over her, forcing her to lean over the table. His large hands slid down her arms, finding her hands and tangling their fingers together. She bucked back against him and his cock slid into her just a fraction, yet it was enough that they sighed in unison.

His breath was hot against her neck, his tongue sweeping out to taste her as he rhythmically arched against her without fully breaching her. Then he pressed her fingers around the leather straps at the middle of the table.

"Hold on," he ordered, closing her fists so that she held the straps.

She obeyed and clung tight. Now she saw why there were restraints here. She could be buckled in, forced to stand the way she was instead of asked to do so. Made to wait as he took his time examining her, bent over the table and ready for his bidding. She felt liquid heat seep from her entrance at just the thought of such a thing.

But he didn't seem interested in waiting or tormenting her tonight. He spread her open from behind and stroked his fingers over her soaked entrance. She heard him growl out satisfaction at her wet, hot state and then he took her.

One thrust, hard and deep, and he was fully seated within her. Her body was so sensitive, so ready that just that one action set off the first tremors of release throughout her body. Beatrice cried out, slamming back as she searched for more, begged for more with her actions.

He gave her what she wanted. He reached around and pinched the hidden bundle of nerves within her folds while at the same time he pulled back and slammed into her body forcefully.

She shattered.

For several blissful moments, her entire being grew focused on the area between her thighs. She didn't care that she was screaming loudly enough to bring down the damned house. She didn't care that she was giving Gareth so much power by letting him see how easily he could control her pleasure. All she cared about was that wave after tremoring wave of complete ecstasy was overtaking her and she never wanted it to end.

But it did. Slowly, she found herself coming out of the haze, her body occasionally twitching with the force of her release. Behind her Gareth pounded on, taking her over and over. He seemed to sense that her climax was over, for he slipped his hands from between her legs and instead covered her breasts, massaging gently as he worked his hips with merciless precision.

The second release surprised her, for Beatrice had never thought she could so quickly lose control again. Her body began to tremble and she let go of the restraints, reaching back to cup Gareth's neck and hold him to her as she was overcome by pleasure once again.

His thrusts became erratic as she sobbed out his name and suddenly he was gone, pulling away from her as she felt the hot spray of his essence splash across her lower back.

They fell forward together across the table and Beatrice shut her eyes in exhaustion and utter, complete satisfaction.

Chapter Eight

eatrice opened her eyes and looked around. She didn't recognize her surroundings and through the bleary haze of sleep, she began to panic. She sat up, rubbing her eyes, only to find she was completely naked.

That was when memory hit her in a few highly detailed bursts. She remembered her arrival, losing her virtue, the highly charged supper with Gareth and then the "tour" to his hidden room of pleasure of vice.

She was back in his chamber now, wrapped in his sheets . . . but she was alone. And she had no idea how she had gotten here. The last thing she recalled was Gareth pressing a few warm kisses along her naked spine.

Gathering the sheets around her, she collected her thoughts. After they made love in his special room, she must have fallen asleep. Certainly the events of the day had exhausted her. If that were true, it meant someone had carried her here. It was possible that someone had been a servant, but in her heart she was certain it had been Gareth.

She shivered. In her sleep, she had been utterly vulnerable. He could have done anything he liked to her body. While she was unaware, she had no idea how long he had looked at her or what he had whispered or even how he had touched her. A shiver moved through her, but she refused to acknowledge any pleasure those thoughts brought her.

She didn't *like* that she had allowed him that kind of power.

She looked at the clock beside the bed. It was after ten in the morning. How long had he been gone? Or had he slept here at all?

Well, it was time to find out. She got up and found that a silken dressing gown had been left for her at the foot of the bed. She stared at the delicate fabric. It wasn't something from her wardrobe, but it was obviously made for a woman of about her size. Had it once belonged to his late wife or perhaps a mistress? Or was it something just for her?

Pursing her lips, Beatrice draped it around her shoulders and went to the bell at the door. As she tugged it to summon a servant to assist her in readying for the day, she took a deep breath.

After a few moments, the door opened and a young maid stepped into the room. She gave Beatrice a nervous smile. "May I help you, miss?"

"I wish to dress and then I want to see Lord Highcroft. And let us hurry it along."

The girl jolted into action and Beatrice sighed as she let her thoughts wander. Today was well and truly the first day of this arrangement and after last night she was beginning to fully understand what that meant, both for her body and for her soul. Gareth wanted something from her that she had never remotely considered sharing.

He wanted everything.

Although she had specifically asked to be taken to Gareth as soon as she was dressed, a footman instead took her to the dining room. She stepped inside and looked around, annoyed to find she was alone.

She turned on the man with a frown. "I told you to take me to your master."

Unlike most servants, this one looked her right in the eye. He didn't seem to fear her, though his gaze held a healthy dose of contempt.

"I do what the marquis asks of me, miss. Not you."

She folded her arms and let out her breath in a huff of outrage, hoping to hide how uncomfortable this situation made her. The other servants pretended not to know that she was Gareth's whore. This one did not. And it was clear he had little respect for her.

"You shall do whatever your betters say," Beatrice snapped. "And you shall remember your place. Now what is your name?"

The man simply glared.

She marched forward, but her heart had begun to throb with anxiety. "You heard me. What is your name?"

"Hodges," came a quiet male voice from the entrance to the dining hall.

Beatrice squeezed her eyes shut as she recognized it as Gareth's. She also heard the deep disapproval in his tone. With a frown, she turned to face him. Gareth stared at her, though he continued to speak to his servant.

"You may go."

The footman hesitated for a moment, but then he nodded his agreement and slipped past his master to disappear into the hallway.

"You should put a tighter leash on your servants," Beatrice said, turning to harshness to cover her discomfort at being caught speaking to his servants in such a way when it was clear he didn't approve. Not to mention the strange thrill that worked through her at being alone with Gareth after last night's shocking events. "For a man who craves control, you have none whatsoever over that one."

Gareth stood in the doorway for a moment and then pushed away and entered the room. He strode to the spread of food laid out for their enjoyment and grabbed a plate from the buffet.

"You are in rare form this morning, aren't you, Beatrice?" he said as he placed a few items on his plate. "A good morning to you, too."

She folded her arms, the heat of embarrassment flooding

her cheeks. "I don't know what you mean by 'rare form,' sir."

Actually, she did, but she wasn't about to admit she had lashed out needlessly at a servant simply because she was uncomfortable. There was no need to explain herself to this or any other man.

"Don't you?" he asked, facing her with an arched brow. "I don't believe you are really so unaware of yourself. You all but attacked my footman, who did nothing to you but took you exactly where I asked him to."

"But *I* asked him to take me to you," she snapped, folding her arms. "I was very specific in my instructions."

"But I pay his salary," Gareth said, his soft and even tone a counterpoint to the tremor in her own.

She pursed her lips, for she had no answer for him. It was exactly as the servant, himself, had said. In truth, until she was marchioness over this house, if that ever indeed happened, there was no reason for any servant to do anything she asked.

Which meant Gareth had more power than she did in one more way.

"Now, will you sit?" he asked, motioning to the seat beside his.

She hesitated, but then her stomach rumbled and she scowled. She did want to eat, so there was no choice. She trudged to the table and sat. To her surprise, Gareth set the plate he had prepared in front of her.

"Would you like tea?" he asked, motioning to the pot in the middle of the table.

She nodded and he poured first for her and then for himself. When he sat down, she took a bite of toast and watched him while she chewed.

"What is that look for?" he asked with a smile.

"I was just thinking, wasn't I supposed to be *your* slave?" She motioned to the food before her. "And yet you are serving me."

"You mistake politeness and care for slavery," he said with another irritating smile. "You are my guest, I wish for you to be comfortable. That has nothing to do with your ultimate surrender in my bedroom."

As much as she wished she could concoct one, Beatrice had very little response to Gareth's quiet claim. At least none that wouldn't make her look even worse than she already did. And for whatever reason, she didn't want Gareth to view her in an even poorer light.

They sat quietly for a while. Gareth sipped his tea and thumbed through a stack of papers from London that had been set at his place before either of them even entered the room. Beatrice picked through her food, enjoying the fresh fruits, perfectly baked pastries and well-done meats his staff had prepared. If she lived here, there was no doubt she would grow fat with such fare.

Through the silence, she waited. She watched. And after a quarter of an hour of comfortable silence had passed, she finally set her fork aside and stared at him.

"You are the most frustrating man in all the country," she snapped.

He lifted his gaze from his paper and stared at her. "How in the world have I transgressed against you now? I have been quietly reading my paper while you had your breakfast. Or do you not approve of *The Highcroft Weekly?* It is a local gazette and I admit it leaves something to be desired in both content and the quality of its writing, but—"

"You know I don't care one bit about your silly paper," Beatrice interrupted with a sigh. "But we have been sitting here for Lord knows how long and you haven't . . ."

He raised his eyebrows in encouragement when she trailed off with a heated blush. "Haven't?"

"You haven't even tried to seduce me!" Beatrice finally huffed out. "Is that not why I am here? To see if we are compatible in a physical way? I somehow doubt that the two tumbles we had yesterday are enough to satisfy your curiosity about the subject. Not after how you built up what you want to such heights of drama."

Gareth leaned back. "Beatrice, do you not think this is a seduction?"

"Of course it isn't!" She tossed her napkin aside and pushed to her feet. "We are sitting having the most mundane morning imaginable. I have sat at my own dining table with my mother like this a thousand times, though granted, it was, blessedly, more quiet here with you."

He did not move, even when she paced away to the closest window in frustration.

"But when you sat with your mother all those times, were you thinking of sex?" he asked mildly.

She turned on him with an outraged gasp. "Of course not."

"And yet this morning you were clearly thinking of seduction, because you spoke of it." He tilted his head. "Were you waiting for me to touch you, perhaps beneath the table? Or to whisper how much I wanted to bury my cock deep inside your pussy?"

Beatrice stiffened. She had never heard that term before, but she could well imagine what he meant from its context.

"Were you?" he pressed.

She jerked out a nod. "Yes. You brought me here for sex. Of course I was thinking about it."

"Then we *are* engaged in a seduction, my dear." He finally pushed to his feet and moved toward her with a lazy possessiveness in his eyes.

Beatrice wanted to turn away from it, but remained rooted in her spot.

"While I sat beside you," he murmured. "All I could think about was the scent of you. It's beginning to seep into me, and just the whiff of your skin makes me hard as a rock. I was watching you as you bent over your plate. Did you know even that slight motion gave me a tiny view of your cleavage in that gown?"

Beatrice looked down with a gasp.

"That little glimpse made me hot to bare your skin and touch you. But part of the seduction is waiting, Beatrice. It's wondering when the moment will come, because that makes the moment all the more enjoyable. Don't you like waiting? Wondering when we will once again melt into the passion we shared last night?"

Beatrice stared at him. He was closer than ever, just a pace's length in front of her. She could feel his body heat, she could smell his skin just as he said he could smell hers. It was exciting and confusing and frustrating all at once.

"I don't know," she admitted as she wet her lips.

He nodded as he reached out to trail just a fingertip down her cheekbone. She wanted to sigh into it, close her eyes, but she refused to show that weakness to him.

"That is very honest. Perhaps the first honest thing you have ever said to me."

She wrinkled her brow. People despised her because she was too honest, didn't they?

"What do you mean?" she asked.

He was damnably calm. "I think you are far less of a shrew than you wish people to believe."

Beatrice flinched. She hated when he implied that he could see more of her than anyone else. The arrogance rankled her. And worse, she feared it might be true. She didn't want him to see more. She didn't want him to know her.

And so she pushed him away the only way she knew how. She blurted out, "Are *you* less of a murderer, my lord?"

The moment she said it, the moment Gareth's eyes went hard as steel, she wished she could take it back. Because it had been a mistake and God knew how she would now pay.

★ ★ ★

Even though Beatrice's sharp words did exactly as she had intended when she said them and cut him to the bone, Gareth did not react. Despite an anger that boiled up within him, he simply stared at her. Even. Focused. He found control and clung to it.

Beatrice turned her face. "Stop looking at me like that," she whispered. He did not reply, but held his gaze steady. She shot him a glare from the corner of her eye. "*Stop!*"

Still, he remained steadfast. He stayed up against her, not allowing her to move, and he stared. Because he knew it would break her more than a thousand retorts could ever do. His focused, undivided attention was more punishment to Beatrice than anything else in the world.

He wanted to know why.

"I–I'm sorry," she finally whispered, shifting uncomfortably. Her eyes darted up and he nodded.

"Thank you," he whispered. Then he tilted his head slightly. "Why are you like this, Beatrice?"

She frowned and for the first time he truly saw her wall come down. The anger, the sharpness, the ferocity bled away, and it left in its wake a sadness that she allowed for only a brief moment.

"I don't know," she finally said. "My father died when I was very young. I suppose it . . . ."

She trailed off as if she didn't know how to finish the sentence. Gareth nodded, thinking of the devastation of his own parents' deaths. Only he had been left with a beloved grandmother who made every effort to ease his pain. Beatrice had been left with only her sisters and a mother who was difficult at best. Somehow he couldn't picture Dorthea Albright offering comfort or sound guidance.

"It must have been difficult for you," he said softly and he took a step back.

She slipped past him in the space he had afforded her and walked away slowly. With her back to him, she said, "It was. I was his princess. When he was gone, I lost everything I knew. Everything I was."

She hesitated and he allowed her whatever thoughts had stopped her. Finally she turned and he actually saw the hardness return to her stare, washing away the vulnerability she had shown him. If anything, she was more distant now than ever before.

"But I am being foolish. That was many years ago and it is unimportant now."

Gareth chose not to argue or push, for it was clear those actions would garner him nothing but more of a fight. He had won his prize already. For the first time since he met her, he had seen something *real* in Beatrice. Something human that she might want to crush, but still lived in her.

She might not want to give that to him, but he could take it. Through her body, he could steal that vulnerability and mold it.

"What is important, then, Beatrice?" he asked softly. He

stepped up behind her at the window and leaned in, letting his body brush hers. She sighed very softly as their bodies touched, but did not answer.

He touched her shoulder and guided her around, pleased that she offered him no resistance. She might not know it, but she was already bending to his will. She leaned against the clean glass, staring up at him with eyes glazed with passion and heat.

"What is important?" he repeated as he slipped his hands up to cover her breasts. She moaned.

"Th—this," she stammered.

He nodded. "And do you want more?"

She bit her lip, her white teeth sinking seductively into the pink flesh. It took everything in him not to smash his mouth to hers.

"Yes," she finally admitted. "I do want more."

He slipped his hands from her breasts and caught her wrists. Without breaking eye contact, he lifted them up until he pinned her back against the window, arms above her head.

Her eyes widened and she looked at him in question and just a tinge of fear. But more than that, there was excitement in her stare. Pure desire that couldn't be denied.

"You will not come until I allow it," he ordered, bending to press his lips behind her ear. "Do you understand? If you orgasm before I tell you yes, you *will* be punished."

She sucked in a breath as he drew back to stare down at her. He could see she wanted to refuse. She wanted to fight.

But just as he hoped, she wanted to come more. She wanted to fuck and that overcame everything else.

"Fine," she said through clenched teeth, but her hips were already rocking against his.

He smiled and dropped his mouth to hers. She lifted her chin, eagerly meeting his lips with parted ones. He took what she offered gently at first, simply enjoying the flavor of her mouth, the taste of tea and sweet jam still lingered. But the longer he kissed her, the less gentle he became. He made his demands with his tongue, driving it deep into her eager mouth, he made more demands with his hips as he arched into her softness and heard the swish of her skirts against glass.

"Gareth," she gasped as his lips left hers to move to her delicate throat. "We should go upstairs. We should—"

He pulled back to look at her. "No one will enter. They have strict instructions."

She cast a quick glance over her shoulder. "But the window . . . someone could see."

"Now, now, my dear," he all but purred. "We have already established that you *like* the idea of someone seeing you . . . or *hearing* your pleasure."

Beatrice gasped and her gaze flitted from his. "Of course not."

"Do not forget about my servant, Beatrice," he whispered. "I certainly have not."

Her cheeks darkened and the flush spread down her neck to her chest.

"Th–that was a momentary weakness."

He moved in for her throat again, murmuring against her skin, "Momentary? No, I think not. In some dark place you've tried so hard to hide, I imagine you can easily picture eyes on you as you come, seeing your pleasure. Wishing they were you. Or *with* you."

She bit her lip and moved her hands against his, but he would not release her.

"This is where I want you, Beatrice," he whispered. "And I think you want me here, as well. Surrender to all the pleasure you know I'll give."

She arched against him with another moan as he bit her earlobe gently. "God, yes."

He didn't ask for more. He released her hands and quickly popped open the buttons along the front of her pretty gown. She shifted to let him push the gown away, followed by her chemise, and bare her breasts.

Her gaze shifted to the dining room entryway, but then she arched in mute offering. He couldn't help but chuckle as he dropped his head to her breast. He swirled his tongue around one hard nipple and reveled in the way her breath caught. She was writhing now, rolling her hips against his as he tugged her tender flesh.

The rest of her dress swished around her ankles as he swept it aside, leaving her nearly naked right there in the dining room. Her backside molded against the glass and she gasped again.

"Cold?" he asked, lifting his mouth away from her breast.

She rolled her head back. "I like it."

His cock twitched at the admission. Damn, but this woman was built for sex and sin, no matter what kind of front she put on. No matter how she resisted, in the end it was in her nature to submit, to yield, to moan and beg for him. Once he had her ultimate surrender, it was going to be sweet.

For now, he would settle for this. He caught her wrists again, this time in one hand and pinned them to the glass. With the other hand he guided her legs open wide and stroked one finger along the entrance to her body. He growled out a sound of pure possession when he found she was wet and ready for him. But not yet. Not yet. He had told her she couldn't come until he gave her permission.

It was time to test the bounds of her obedience. He spread her open, peeling the folds of flesh back until the wet pearl of her clit sparkled up at him. He licked his thumb and then lightly caressed the hard nub of flesh.

Immediately her hips twitched and she sighed out a gasp of surprised, intense pleasure. Already she was on the brink.

"Don't forget what you promised, Beatrice," he whispered. "You shall not come until you have my permission."

She whimpered in response but she didn't draw back or argue. Another step toward his ultimate plans for her. He stroked her slit again, gathering some of her own juices to lubricate her clit with another gentle pinch.

"It feels so good," she whispered, her voice trembling. "I want—I want—"

"You want to come," he murmured, slipping a finger into her sheath and stroking her with one smooth thrust.

She nodded as she arched against his touch.

"Ask me," he said, ceasing all movement and catching her eye.

She stared at him, her lips trembling, her legs shaking from need and desire. Her sheath fluttered, but she wasn't experienced enough yet to know that squeezing around him could help her gain release without his assistance. Or that rubbing against his poised thumb could relieve her. Later she would know these things, but she wouldn't do them because he told her not to. He had no doubt she would eventually be mastered.

"Ask," he repeated.

"Please," she whispered, high color darkening her cheeks. "Please let me . . ."

She opened and shut her mouth, searching for the word to describe her release.

"Come," he said when she hesitated. "You want to come."

"I want to come," she sobbed. "I want you to make me come. Please let me."

"How?" he whispered, the sweet torment testing him as much as he tested her. "With my fingers, my mouth or my cock?"

She groaned. "Your—your mouth," she gasped.

He arched a brow, taken aback by her answer. He hadn't expected it so quickly and with such fervor.

"You liked it when I tongued your clit?" he said as he let go of her wrists and slid down her body, suckling her bare skin along the way. "You liked it when I tasted your release?"

"Yes," she cried as he blew out a breath against her sheath. "Yes, I liked it. Please, let me have that again."

"Wait," he reminded her. "Wait for me to tell you when."

She jerked out a nod. Now that her hands were free, she tangled one in his hair, but the other rested against the window behind her, fingers curling and opening against the glass in hopeless fists as she waited and tried to control her trembling body.

He pressed a kiss to her outer lips gently, then opened her. His tongue came out and he lapped her clit just once. She yelped a sound of pleasure and her fingers tightened in his hair.

He drove his tongue inside of her, tasting her desire, scenting how close she was to utter explosion, but not ready to allow it yet. He wanted her to depend on him for the permission. To wait, as he had ordered, even though it went against her body's needs and her own mind.

"Not yet," he whispered against her skin.

She tensed and he felt her grappling for control, reaching for some kind of sanity even as he licked and sucked her closer to oblivion. Finally, he returned to her clit. He sucked it once and she bucked, but to her credit she did not surrender to her own desires. She followed his order.

The second time, he felt her sheath begin to quiver and he knew she was at the brink. In a moment, she wouldn't have a choice, she would come whether she tried to stop it or not.

"Now," he said. "Come for me, Beatrice."

She cried out when he suckled her again and the explosion of her orgasm was intense and enormous. Her hips rocked out of control, her sheath twitched and shuddered.

He stood up even as she continued to arch and sway with relief and shucked his trousers down. She opened for him even as she continued to cry out and took him when he thrust into her in one stroke.

"Keep coming, angel," he whispered into her shoulder as he retreated and moved forward again.

She sobbed with pleasure, her nails digging into his shoulders through his jacket. Her legs tightened around him and her hips ground as the orgasm he had started with his lips continued on.

He took her. There was no doubt that was what he was doing. His strokes were hard and harsh. But she didn't resist. She met each one with enthusiasm, abandoning herself to him utterly and completely.

Her surrender was so sweet that it drove him to the edge of orgasm within a few thrusts. He could feel her body's pleasure fading, her limbs relaxing after such intense release. He wanted to feel her come with him. He wanted to take her even further along the road to being under his sexual sway.

"Did I tell you to stop?" he asked, his voice low against her ear.

She tensed, leaning back to look at him with an unreadable expression. "I—"

"I want you to come again," he murmured, grinding his hips against hers in a slow circle.

Her lids fluttered shut and she moaned. "I can't do it again."

"You can," he said, repeating the slow circle as he cupped her backside with one hand and lifted her into a better position.

He slipped his other hand between their bodies, squeezing one breast gently before he snaked his way down between her legs. He thrust forward as he fingered her sensitive clit.

"More to the point, you *will* come, Beatrice."

Her breath came in pants now as she rested her head back against the glass behind her. She whimpered as he thrust again.

"It's too much," she moaned.

He chuckled and stimulated her clit once more. "There is no such thing. Come for me. *Now*."

With a cry, she did exactly what he had ordered. Her hips arched in a wild rhythm against his and her cries filled the air as her body squeezed his cock in steady, wild pulses.

His wire-thin control snapped as her fingers dug into his lower arms and he growled out his own pleasure before he pulled out of her and let his seed pulse between them as his arms came around her.

She had done as he asked and he had reveled in every moment of it. If he had been skeptical of their arrangement before, now he was beginning to wonder if he had been wrong. Perhaps he *had* found the woman who could accept his proclivities, his life.

Perhaps he had found his bride after all.

Chapter Nine

Beatrice lifted her face to the sunny sky and drew in a deep breath. After days hiding away in Gareth's estate, the feel of the breeze in her hair and the sun on her skin was heavenly. She continued walking down the rolling hill away from the house.

It wasn't that she was complaining about what she had been doing since her arrival here. On the contrary, locking herself away and giving her body to Gareth was most definitely her pleasure. In the four days she had been here, his touch had brought her to completion so many times and in so many ways that she had almost lost count. And yet, she still waited for him to bring her back to that secret room she had seen on her first night here.

She still waited for him to take his control of her body

beyond just the control of her orgasms, which he had perfected to near art. Now just the sound of his gravelly voice murmuring, "Now," could make her quiver. If he so much as added his touch, she was lost.

But she was well aware that he had more for her to bear and she found herself tightly wound with tension . . . and titillation . . . at the idea that he would soon require more and more from her body . . . from her soul.

Still, she welcomed this respite from the intensity of her time in Gareth's bed. He had been obliged to take care of some business and she had decided to walk through the rolling hills and get to know the land better.

She breathed in the softly scented air and looked around her. Gareth's estate was the most beautiful place she had ever seen. Her own childhood estate had been in terrible disarray her entire life. In the end, their furniture had been shabby and ill kept, her father had sold many of their finer things. It was humiliating.

London was better. The townhome Beatrice shared with her mother and sister was very nice. Of course it would be. It had been provided by the shared funds of her two very rich brothers-in-law, and they spared no expense to make it appear that they gave a damn. But as fine a home as it was, it was so close and tight to its neighbors that there was no freedom to be found there.

As for her married sisters' estates, no one could deny that the Earl of Rothschild and the Duke of Kilgrath had magnificent homes, but she never felt quite right at either of them.

From the moment she stepped within their walls, she knew her hosts were counting the moments until she was gone. No amount of false friendliness or beauty could camouflage that fact.

Here it was different. Here she could breathe. There was no mother standing over her shoulder giving her twenty-five directions on what she should do differently. Here she did not have eyes on her, constantly judging and hating her for things she had done and said. She felt free as she walked along the pretty lawn that seemed to go on forever.

Even in the house, she *belonged*. Aside from the one footman who seemed to personally despise her ever since that morning when she berated him, the servants did not treat her badly or openly judge her. The house was available to her and her desires, whether that was a quiet hour reading in Gareth's library or a hot, passionate tryst with him against the door in his tidy office.

She shivered as she shook off that particular memory. Yes, she *did* feel comfortable here. At home. Perhaps, if she passed all of Gareth's tests and they married as they had agreed to do at the beginning of their bargain, she could even be *happy*. Which was a concept she had all but given up on over the past few years.

She sighed as she entered a little copse of trees at the base of a hill. One had been felled by a storm what looked like years ago and she sank down on the fallen trunk to relax for a moment before she returned to the house and a planned meeting with Gareth after he concluded his business.

She had just taken her place and arranged her skirts around her when there was a rustling in the woods off to her right. She tensed as she looked through the shadowy branches.

"H–hello?" she called out into the quiet, feeling foolish since she realized the sound was likely only some small animal hunting in the brush. Still, she sensed a presence here. A person.

There was no reply of course, and she shook her head at her own foolish imagination's wild creation. Obviously, she had been cooped up in the house too long. Perhaps she would suggest to Gareth that they take a walk each day, although she wasn't certain she wanted so much time with Gareth when he could interrogate her about the past she wanted to keep secret. He wanted to know too much, to see—

Before she could finish her thought, the rustling came again, this time louder, and she was certain it came from something much larger than a field mouse or rabbit nosing through the brush. She got to her feet and faced the sound.

"Who is there?" she snapped, retreating once again to sharpness when fear mobbed her. She knew better than to show any weakness to an enemy. "I know someone is out there. Show your face to me immediately."

"With pleasure."

Beatrice yelped as a man stepped out of the shadows toward her. He was tall and thin, rangy, almost like he hadn't been eating well for quite some time. His clothing was in ill repair, as well. He held a bottle in one hand, but even before she recognized it as whiskey, she smelled the brew on him and recoiled.

"And just who are you, trespassing on the Marquis of Highcroft's estate?" she asked, backing up as she tried to maintain a haughty, angry tone in the face of this marauding stranger who was staring at her with such focused intent.

He laughed, though the sound held no pleasure. "*He* said Highcroft had a whore here with him, but here you are, a *fine lady*."

Beatrice flinched at his tone, filled with bitterness and hatred. His pointed, insulting words hung between them, making her stomach turn and her hands shake. This person apparently despised her, though she was certain she had never met him before he popped out of the woods behind her.

Worse, the stranger before her said "he" had told him something about her. "He," another person . . . someone spreading the word about her residence here. If that were true, if someone had seen her arrive here, if Gareth's servants were spreading tales in the township, that meant those stories could get back to the *ton* at large and there would be no going back then. Her life would be utterly and completely over.

"I don't know what you are talking about," she snapped, as she took several steps away from the drunken invader. She had to control whatever damage had been done by what he heard and then get away from this person as quickly as possible. "I am Lord Highcroft's fiancée and I'm here with a large party of guests. You, sir, are not one of them and I suggest you leave immediately."

The man had stopped advancing on her and the bottle in his hand hit the ground at his feet as he stared at her. High emotion filled his cloudy stare, but this time it wasn't hatred but shock and perhaps a tinge of heartache.

"*Fiancée*, are you?" His voice cracked slightly. "She's dead in the ground and he replaces her with some tart."

Beatrice folded her arms, stung and ever more frightened by this person's words and his obviously emotional state. "If you do not go at once, I shall scream and it will bring our party running. They are only just over the hill."

The man shook off his thoughts and smiled at her. "There isn't anyone close by, miss. I know that for a fact. Just as I know there isn't a party here at all. It's just *you* and *him* and whatever dirty little game he wants you to play."

Beatrice opened and shut her mouth hopelessly. This was worse than she thought. This man had more than a passing rumor, he had details about why she was here. Someone with intimate knowledge *had* apparently told him about her. That idea sickened and frightened her.

She had to get away. To return to Gareth. He would know what to do.

She lifted her chin with all the haughtiness she had ever used to push others away. "I have heard enough of your insults. I'm returning to the house, sir. I once again advise you to leave!"

She turned, but he bounded forward and caught her arm. Instinct immediately took over and Beatrice began to fight, pushing at her captor's hand, yanking her arm to free it until it hurt, but he held fast all the time.

"Oh, no you don't," he cried as she struggled. "You and I aren't finished. I won't let him get away with this. With anything."

"Stop it," Beatrice screamed as the vagrant spun her around to face him. The whiskey smell was stronger now and she leaned away from it. "Release me this instant."

He didn't, instead he stepped back and began dragging her deeper into the wooded darkness and God only knew what kind of torment. She screamed as loudly as she could, but had no illusion her cries would bring aid. She had refused the company of the servant Gareth provided her, so she had not been followed. No one would even notice she was missing until she was late for her meeting with Gareth in almost an hour. By that time she could very well be dead.

So she did the only thing she could think of. Pivoting slightly, she kneed her attacker right between the legs as hard as she could.

He let her go as he let out a guttural groan of pure pain. "You bitch!"

"Beatrice!" came a voice from the distance.

She turned and ran toward it, recognizing Gareth's voice instantly. "I'm here! Help me!" she cried as she saw him come over the hill toward her. When he heard her call out, he began to run to meet her.

"What is it?" he asked as she launched herself into his arms and held tight, her body trembling even as she willed it to stop. "Why were you screaming?"

"He appeared out of nowhere," she said, pointing toward

the man who was just now rising to his feet and weaving toward them. "He attacked me!"

Gareth set her aside gently and crashed toward the unknown assailant like an angry beast freed from his cage. "What the hell—"

He did not finish. To Beatrice's surprise, when the other man lifted his head and looked at Gareth, it stopped Gareth in his tracks. He stared and the two men locked eyes. From the look they exchanged, it was evident they knew each other.

"What are you doing here?" Gareth breathed.

The other man shook his head. "It won't happen, Highcroft. I swear to the heavens, I'll do to her what you did to mine. I swear to it."

Then he turned and ran off through the woods. Well, limped off, since he was still clutching his crotch. It gave Beatrice some small satisfaction to know that she had damaged him. But it was *very* small since his final threat was obviously meant for her.

Gareth seemed to consider making chase, but then he turned back. They stared at each other for a long moment, but then he ran for her and caught her into an embrace again. This time it was far tighter. Far more intense and intimate.

"Are you all right?" he breathed into her hair. "Did he harm you in any way?"

She clung to him, taking comfort in his touch even though she knew she should push away. Flee this emotional connection she so feared making.

"He didn't hurt me." She smiled as she pulled back, but it was shaky at best. "I *did* hurt him."

He returned the shaky smile with one of his own. "You were so brave, Beatrice."

Then his mouth was on her with a desperate fear she could almost taste. She recognized in that moment just how threatened she had been and it frightened her. But with Gareth's arms around her she was safe. Protected. She surrendered to that feeling as they dropped to the ground on their knees at the same time.

She reached for his jacket, shoving at the heavy fabric with both hands, desperate to feel his bare skin on hers. He drew back with surprise lighting his stare.

"Are you certain?"

Instead of words, she responded by cupping his cheeks and lifting herself to kiss him. She poured all of herself into the passion of that kiss and she felt him accept it, felt it merge with his own high emotions. Then he was unbuttoning her gown, she was tearing violently at his shirt. Clothing fell around them, creating a makeshift bed that he lay across, with her splayed across his chest.

His fingers threaded through her hair and the blond length of it fell down around her shoulders and back. She ignored the tickle and instead pressed a warm kiss against Gareth's chest. He growled with pleasure, but to her surprise he didn't control what she did next. He simply pressed one hand into the small of her back to lazily stroke patterns into her skin with his fingers. The other hand he rested behind his head as a pillow.

And all he did was watch her.

She wrinkled her brow. He had never allowed her to control their lovemaking. She wasn't even sure what to do, although her body had some very specific ideas.

"Why are you looking at me like that?" he whispered as he stroked that little hollow in her lower back gently and stoked the fire between her legs without even trying.

"Because you're not . . . not . . ."

"Dominating you?" he asked with a smile.

She nodded.

"If I am to master you, what it truly means is that I take responsibility not just for your pleasure when we make love, but your *needs*. And I think after your ordeal, what you need is to take a little of your power back. So take it, Beatrice. I offer it to you freely."

She blinked. She had never imagined that he considered part of his duty to be the caretaker of her well-being. That implied that he would care for her. Truly consider her needs. The last man who had promised to do that was her father, and he had failed in his charge miserably, leaving Beatrice to vow never to let herself fully depend upon anyone else again.

But Gareth was promising she could. With her body. With more than that. The idea was too intense and she shifted to pull away, but he increased the pressure on her skin and easily kept her splayed atop him.

"Don't run, Beatrice." He held her gaze. "You can overthink this later. You can give me all your reasons for why I am wrong and you are right. For now, take what I'm offering. You need it."

She hesitated as she stared down at him. She *did* want what he offered so desperately. She wanted to be comforted and protected by his touch. She wanted the pleasure she would surely find. And she was tempted by the prospect that the power was shifting in her direction and she could lead where this encounter would take them.

Tentative, she bent her head and pressed her lips to his. She waited for him to overpower with his kiss, but true to his word, he let her lead. He parted his lips, but did not crush or take or claim. She tasted him, resistance melting from her very bones as she surrendered into the kiss and all the pleasure it gave her.

Clearly, it gave him pleasure, too, for she felt his erection press between their bodies, hardening against her outer thigh. She shivered as she slipped a hand down his chest, between their bodies to cup his cock. She stroked him from base to head a few times, loving the velvety hardness of his flesh. He let out a strangled groan at the touch and she reveled in the fact that he got harder for her. *Because* of her.

He tensed at her touch, the vein in his neck pulsing as he let out a guttural moan of pure pleasure. Power surged within her and she shifted over him to straddle his hips. His cock rubbed her belly, but she didn't take him inside of her. Not yet. She kept him in hand, tormenting him with her fingers as she kept her gaze fully locked on him.

He didn't flinch away. If anything, his focus on her grew clearer every time she touched him, like he was giving her more and more of himself, freely and without hesitation. She was in awe of that ability to surrender. In awe and a little frightened. She did not want this connection she felt to him in that moment. She didn't want the warmth in her body that had nothing to do with sex or pleasure, but with emotion.

She had to stop it. She had to make certain that sex remained just that. Sex. Not feeling. Not emotion. Just two bodies coming together.

Without preamble, she shifted up his body and positioned his cock against her wet and ready sheath. With one hard downward thrust she took him fully into her body. They released a mutual moan of pleasure at the joining.

He slipped his warm hand to her breast, teasing her nipples with his fingers as she began to rock her hips over his. Pleasure arced like lightning from his touch to her clit and she found her hips grinding down harder over him, seeking stimulation and pleasure that was easily found in his body.

Already her sheath fluttered and twitched the edge of release, but she couldn't quite find it. She rode harder, loving the buildup to orgasm, but frustrated by her lack of ability to find it. Finally, she sobbed out a sound of upset.

"I can't," she muttered, keeping her gaze away from his. She was weak for wanting release so badly.

"Relax," he soothed, stroking her skin gently. "You'll find it."

"I can't without . . ." She trailed off, hating herself for the power she was about to admit she had lost. "I can't without you saying I should."

She darted her gaze to him and found he was staring at her, not in triumph or power as she had feared. He was looking at her in utter awe. Slowly, he sat up. Instinctively, she wrapped her legs behind his back. They were face to face now, more intimate than at any time they'd made love before, because there was no turning away.

He tilted his head and they kissed just as he began to lift into her. She met his strokes, grinding against him as the pleasure she had lost returned to her body with intensive, blinding speed. She tilted her head back with a cry as her entire body joined in the pleasure.

Finally he whispered, "Come, Beatrice. Give me your pleasure."

Just as she feared, the permission was what her aching body needed. Instantly, the release she'd been reaching for mobbed her with pleasure so intense it was almost pain. She lost control of her body, her movements becoming wild as she rode Gareth's cock with abandon. Yet he didn't let her become totally lost. He held her, kissing her through the crisis and murmuring sweet words that blurred into her pleasure and made it all the better.

Finally, he tilted his head back, neck straining, body trembling. A few more rapid thrusts and he exploded, this time within her body, pumping heat and pleasure and strength into her in a splash of wet seed that only seemed to stimulate her further and take her to a new plane of pleasure and relief.

After what seemed like an eternity, the shivering, quaking pleasure ended, and Beatrice came back to reality. She remembered they were outside, arms and legs tangled, their sweaty foreheads gently pressed together and their breathing in tandem. Somehow she had forgotten that, forgotten everything else but him.

She leaned back to look at him and felt something she had never expected when she began this bargain with him.

In some way she had bonded with him. And as much as she feared that, as much as she hated that she had completely given the control of her body's pleasure to him . . . it also gave her a sense of peace.

And peace was not something Beatrice was accustomed to.

Chapter Ten

Gareth watched as Beatrice slowly shimmied her chemise over her head and smoothed the fabric over her skin. Just that simple act aroused him beyond reason, and he had the strong urge to lay her back across the grass and take all the pleasure and warmth he could from her pale flesh.

But he didn't, because so much had changed in just a few hours. He had felt the shift as they made love, but the new understanding between them had been voiced perfectly when Beatrice admitted she needed his permission to find her orgasm. That was a powerful declaration from this woman who wanted to be in control of everything and would lash out if someone threatened her power.

Deeper than that, even, was the fact that he had spent his seed inside her sheath. He hadn't planned that moment of abandon, it had simply happened naturally as they reveled in ultimate passion and release.

Still, that one moment's weakness changed everything. Gareth was many things, but he would not sire a bastard. There was a chance of a baby now, which sealed their future as a married couple even before he had fully tested her ability to surrender to his lifestyle.

She faced him as she gathered up her dress from the grass and Gareth's pleasant but confusing thoughts faded. He frowned as he saw the faint black stain of a bruise lashed across her arm. And it wasn't a mark made from his passion. No, the grip of her attacker had done that.

An attacker who had come here because of *him*.

"My God, Beatrice," he breathed as he reached out to trace the faint mark.

She glanced at the bruise and a shadow of fear crossed her face even though she said, "'Tis nothing. It will be gone in a few days."

He shook his head. "I owe you my deepest apologies for what you endured today. I have lived on this estate for many years. I am afraid my comfort with the place led me to be complacent. I never would have let you roam the estate alone if I had believed—"

To his surprise her normally tense face softened. "Of course you wouldn't. I don't blame you for what happened today," she soothed him.

Then she seemed to recognize how much emotion she was sharing, for she turned away abruptly. Without looking at him, she stepped into her gown and quickly fastened the buttons along the front. Keeping her back to him, she began to comb through her long blond hair with her fingers. It was a completely ordinary motion, but he recognized that it was her way of keeping him at arm's length.

"When you approached the man who confronted me in the woods," she said softly. "You seemed to recognize each other. Who was he?"

Gareth stiffened and finished buttoning his own shirt before he answered her perfectly legitimate question. He didn't wish to share the truth, but after what had happened, he owed it to her. If she was being threatened, she deserved to know by whom.

And why.

He cleared his throat. "The man who attacked you was . . . he was my late wife's brother."

That stopped her from fussing with her hair. Slowly, she turned to face him and her skin had grown even more pale than normal.

"H–his threats," she finally said after a long, uncomfortable pause. "He said he would do to me what you did to *her*. He meant his sister, didn't he? Your late wife."

When he nodded, she shivered. He realized she was thinking of death. Worse, of murder. That ugly thing that had hung over him for years. The accusation Beatrice had never seemed to put much credence in, even from the first moment she met him. Perhaps she was the only one.

But now he saw doubt flicker in her stare, and he was taken aback by how much that doubt troubled him.

He cleared his throat, and this time it was he who turned away so she wouldn't see his reaction.

"Laurel's family has been very angry with me since her death, and perhaps I deserve their wrath, for she is lost to them forever."

He shook his head as he thought of how rabid Laurel's brother, Adam, had looked when he had Beatrice in his sights. That memory inspired a protective rage in him that was almost overpowering. The idea that the man would take some kind of twisted vengeance on her . . . well, it brought a veil of red fury down over Gareth's eyes.

"I never thought he would go so far," he murmured as he tried to control his emotions.

When she didn't respond, Gareth turned to find Beatrice was still standing in the same spot she had been when they began this conversation, but all her fluttering with clothing and hair had stopped. She simply stared at him, and perhaps for the first time she didn't try to mask her perusal.

She clenched her hands in front of her and he could see they were shaking.

"I want to ask you a question," she whispered, her voice breaking, and he prayed it wasn't in terror.

He nodded, for he knew what she was going to ask even before she continued.

"Gareth, did . . . *did* you kill your wife?"

He had been prepared for those words, but they hit him like a punch to the gut nonetheless. That question was the one that had haunted him for two long years. The worst part was he wasn't certain of the answer. Some nights he felt like a murderer as he lay in his bed reliving the events of that horrible day Laurel's life was snuffed out.

"Gareth . . ." she whispered when he didn't answer.

He paced away, not wanting to explain, to say out loud what he had done, what his wife had done and why. The why was the worst part . . . especially for Beatrice.

"It's more complicated than that," he said.

She strode after him and caught his arm. When she tugged, he obliged her by turning to face her. Her blue eyes snapped with anger and worry and fear as she stared up at him.

"Then explain it to me," she said.

He was surprised that for once the sharpness and accusation of her tone was not present. The hard edge Beatrice used as a shield had vanished, leaving her just a woman who wanted—no, *needed*—to know the truth.

"Gareth," she whispered. "Someone attacked me today in the name of a woman I have no idea about beyond rumor and conjecture. And you and I are entered into a bargain that we have stated will result in our marriage if we come to an agreement. The very least I deserve is to hear what happened to her. To Laurel." She hesitated and he saw her jaw tighten. "Please."

Gareth drew back. If he had learned anything about the woman standing before him, it was that she didn't *request* anything easily. Demand was more her style, so the fact that she had *asked* him to reveal the truth held a great deal of power to it.

He nodded. "Yes, you deserve that. To understand today's events, I must go back to the beginning."

Beatrice nodded silently.

He shook his head as memory assaulted him. "I—I saw Laurel across a room almost three years ago and in an instant I wanted her."

Beatrice didn't move, but Gareth thought he saw a muscle in her jaw twitch like she didn't like to hear that. He ignored her indication of jealousy and continued.

"I made every effort to meet her. When I did, I fear I could not hide how much I wanted her, but my ardor didn't seem to frighten her. I thought she wanted me just as much, for she allowed me to steal a most passionate kiss in the garden that night. It became clear to all that I wished to court her, but her family strenuously and vocally objected to any match between us. We had long been neighbors, you see, and I think they had heard rumors of what I . . ." He arched a brow in Beatrice's direction. "Well, they probably believed I was somewhat of a libertine."

She nodded and he could see she understood he was referring to the proclivities he possessed. "Still, you married her regardless of their thoughts on the matter."

"You probably noticed the attire of the man who attacked you—Adam is his name." Gareth shrugged. "Laurel's family was in the beginnings of dire financial straits. Her brother Adam inherited a great amount of debt when their father died. And the young man was a drinker and a gambler, himself. I'm afraid I took advantage of those things in my quest to obtain what I desired. Soon, her family had no choice but to agree to a marriage contract, so Laurel and I were wed."

Beatrice nodded. "I was never close to your wife, but I did vaguely know her during her coming-out year, which I believe was the year you wed. There was much mumbling and talk about your quick marriage."

Gareth shook his head. "I knew our quick union caused some damage to her standing, but in truth I didn't care. I was driven to possess her at all costs. Perhaps selfishly driven in more ways than one."

He took a moment to draw breath and regain his composure. To his surprise, Beatrice did not attempt to interrupt or encourage him to continue. She simply waited with a patience he hadn't realized she possessed.

Finally, he continued, "Right after the wedding, I brought her here, where we could spend the first months of our marriage in complete intimacy and privacy. At first, I thought all would be well. Although she was timid with her affections, she seemed somewhat open to lessons in desire and passion. But after a few weeks, I wanted more."

Beatrice watched him pace around the grassy area restlessly. "You wanted her to allow you to dominate her. You wanted her utter surrender, just as you require mine."

He nodded. "That is my nature when it comes to the bedroom, Beatrice. Without dominance, I soon bore of my partner. I did not wish to bore of my wife, so I asked her to give herself over to me. But she—"

He broke off as he thought of Laurel's disgust the first

time he showed her his private pleasure chamber. She had recoiled physically and emotionally. Her voice had been so sharp when she declared she didn't want that room just down the hall from where she slept and would one day raise children. He had tried to reason with her, but she had run away. For three long days she hadn't so much as spoken to him.

He should have known then and let her go. But he hadn't.

"It became more than evident that she didn't want to share my life," he finished with difficulty. "She couldn't stand it, and she didn't even want to try. After our first row on the subject, she would only lie as still as a board in our bed, just bearing my hands on her. There was not even the pretense of enjoyment from her, no matter how patient or accommodating I was. And soon she would not even grant me the barest of intimacy. For months we did not sleep in the same bed and she flinched when I came near her."

Beatrice moved forward a step, her unwavering stare focused on his face. "That is why you are so adamant about 'testing' me. That is why you said we must know if we are compatible before we wed."

He nodded, pain mobbing him just as memory did. If only he had explained his needs to Laurel before they wed, perhaps all that had occurred later could have been avoided.

"But what happened to her, Gareth?" Beatrice asked, her voice hardly above a whisper. "What took you from a passionless marriage no different from many others in the *ton* to her untimely death?"

He swallowed hard. "I did not handle our situation with much finesse, I am afraid. I grew frustrated by her refusal to even try to make our marriage work. As the weeks and months went by, she locked herself away with increasing frequency. When we did speak, it was often to argue. She seemed to become more and more hysterical, even lashing out at me physically from time to time."

Beatrice's eyes went wide with surprise, but she did not interrupt him.

"One night the fighting became unmanageable. Laurel was screaming down the house, despite the fact that I had a friend in residence, despite the fact that the servants and half the county could hear her rail against me."

Beatrice winced and Gareth looked away. It was amazing how simply saying out loud all that had occurred could bring back the emotions of that horrible night.

"The more she went on, the angrier and more frustrated I became," he mused, the clarity of his thoughts almost painful. "Finally, I snapped."

A gasp escaped Beatrice's lips and Gareth looked up at her with a start. He lifted his hands in mute entreaty for understanding and faith.

"I did not touch her, I swear to you! I simply reminded her that she owed me a child, an heir. That by keeping her body from me, she was stealing my legacy and I would not have it any longer."

Beatrice's face relaxed a fraction. "And how did she respond?"

Gareth swallowed, because the dreaded words were caught in his throat. "Apparently, the idea of carrying my sons was utterly distasteful to her. The terror on her face was evidence of her feelings. She clutched at her belly and told me that no child of hers would ever come under my control."

Again, he hesitated, almost physically unable to continue. "Th—then she turned and threw herself down the main staircase."

Beatrice made a strangled sound and lifted her fingers to cover her mouth. She stared at him, her bright blue eyes dark with horror.

"It—it is so high," she finally whispered.

He nodded as nausea hit him in waves just as powerful as they had been that horrible night.

"She fell all the way down, head over heels, and hit the marble floor at the bottom with the worst crash I've ever heard. I rushed to her, but I could see she was dead before I even got to her. Her neck was broken and she was gone. And I, in the eyes of many, was a murderer."

Although he did not want to, Gareth forced himself to look at Beatrice, to see her disgust and her fear as she, too, decided that he was a depraved killer. But when he looked at her he found she was already staring at him, just as he had stared at her earlier. Her blue eyes focused on him with unrelenting attention, but he could not read her emotions, her response to what he had told her.

He shifted under her scrutiny, but made himself take it.

He had known she might be horrified when she learned the truth, he was ready for any reaction.

Except the one she gave. Slowly, Beatrice moved toward him. She reached out and then her fingers curled around his wrist gently.

"Gareth," she whispered. "I—I have never been good at offering comfort—"

He tugged away from her. "I don't want your sympathy, damn it."

"I don't offer that!" she snapped as she grabbed for him again. "I hate to receive it, why would I insult you by giving it? No, I said *comfort*."

Gareth's brow wrinkled. "How can I have comfort? My wife is dead and what I am killed her."

"Stop it." Beatrice's grip on his hands grew tighter. "I cannot stand pity in any form, including the kind turned toward self. It changes nothing. You must know that you did *not* kill her."

He shrugged. "I don't know anything."

"How can you not?" she asked in exasperation. "You did not push her, you didn't even tell her to jump! She did those things of her own volition and for her own reasons."

"Her own reasons were *me*," Gareth insisted. "If she had not married me, if she hadn't been so thoroughly disgusted by what I am, she never would have thrown herself down those stairs. Does it not follow, then, that marrying me killed her?"

"Of course not!" Beatrice barked and it was clear she felt

she'd heard nothing so foolish before. "It just as easily follows that if she had tried to be what you desired, even a little, you two could have come to an understanding. By that logic, Laurel's own inability to compromise is what brought her end. Whatever the cause, the fact is that you have locked yourself away for so long, Gareth. You have allowed the *ton* their whispers and cruelty . . . You have never once defended yourself."

He nodded. "I didn't want to make her memory more sordid than it already was. If those in her family and Society believed me the villain, then it followed that they see her as the victim. It was better than the alternative."

She shook her head. "I don't believe that. Lying to protect her memory, all the while tormenting yourself about what she did for two long years is not *better*. But either way—it is *enough*."

Beatrice met his eyes and again he was taken aback by the unexpected softness in her stare. She truly wished to help him, comfort him, even though it wasn't her nature to nurture. And yet it meant even more to him because it was something she *chose* to do.

"You have punished yourself and allowed others to punish you," she whispered. "Let it be enough now, Gareth."

"That is what Vincent says."

She wrinkled her brow. "Vincent?"

"My best friend, Vincent, the Viscount Knighthill. He was the one visiting us when she took her life. He has long encouraged me to defend myself publicly."

Beatrice put her hands on her hips. "Then I look forward to meeting him, for he sounds like a reasonable fellow with sound advice."

"You shall meet him," Gareth said. "I want to send word for him to come here straightaway."

She tilted her head. "Why?"

"If someone is threatening you, I want a friend close by whom I can trust to help me protect you." Gareth held her stare. "I defend my own."

She shivered at the claim and he smothered a smile. He found he rather liked when she turned her fire and brimstone to the task of protecting him rather than pushing away anyone who dared come near. That kind of fierce protectiveness would make her a good wife, an excellent mother . . . and a tremendous friend.

As if she sensed his thoughts, she blushed and took a step backward, distancing herself from him and from the intensity of this exchange. She folded her arms in front of her and held his stare.

"I am glad you told me about your late wife, Gareth," she said. "Now that I know, our entire situation makes more sense. But—"

He arched a brow, were there to be consequences for what he had confessed, even though she claimed understanding?

"But?" he asked.

She smoothed her gown reflexively. "This *thing* between us has nothing to do with her. I don't want what we do and what we share to have anything to do with what came before."

Gareth blinked. He hadn't been expecting that statement, yet he could readily agree. The truth was, he had asked for this bargain with thoughts of Laurel's refusal in his mind. But from the first moment he touched Beatrice, his late wife hadn't entered his mind. The two women were wholly separate.

And he intended to keep it that way.

"You are right," he said softly. "And I swear to you that my late wife does not and shall not ever enter the bedroom with us."

Beatrice straightened her shoulders. "I am finished with games, Gareth. I have been waiting for you to show me exactly what you want from me and now I demand it."

"*You* demand it?" he said, humor filling him for the first time since he found Adam stalking her.

She nodded, but he sensed her nervousness when she swallowed hard. "Take me back to that special room you showed me the night of my arrival. But this time, I want you to truly give me everything you desire, take everything you need."

He hesitated. Her demand was utter temptation, her offer of complete freedom to do as he wished a gift unlike any other.

"I am not certain you know what you are asking," he said softly.

She held his gaze with no hesitation. "Perhaps not, but we are at a crossroads, Gareth. Decisions must be made, futures must be determined. And this is the only way we will ever know if we are truly compatible."

Gareth let his breath out in a whoosh. He had been easing Beatrice into submission in the hopes that he could coax her. But he realized now, as he stared at her, with her bottom lip trembling and flushed skin, that he had been treating her like Laurel. Hoping for surrender rather than taking it. And fearing her reaction.

But Beatrice was not his late wife. She was stronger, more equipped to take what he desired, even if her nature fought it. Subtlety would never work. Beatrice wanted and needed a firm hand.

And he was more than happy to provide it. Now.

Chapter Eleven

*B*eatrice stood in the dark, sensual pleasure room she had been dreaming about since her arrival at Gareth's estate. Her heart throbbed as she watched him enter the chamber and close the door behind him. As he locked the door, fear tickled at her, but she shoved it aside.

This was what she needed to do. And after the events of today she knew without hesitation that Gareth would not hurt her.

She stared at him. He remained by the door, simply watching her. He seemed as hesitant as she felt, but now she understood why. He feared her reaction when he shed his gentlemanly façade and showed her the dominance he so craved. Laurel had done that to him. The wife he had protected to a fault even as she spurned him.

Empathy swelled in Beatrice, but she forced it aside to pack it away with her fear.

Deeper feelings had no place in this room or with this man. She wanted the freedom he represented, nothing more. Surrender was the way to get it. There might be pleasure, but she could go no further. She already knew the consequences of developing an attachment.

"Remove your clothing," Gareth said. His voice sounded different, more powerful, infinitely more seductive.

And yet she bristled, for his words were an order. Her natural reaction was to tell him to go to the devil and run as far as she could. Instead, she remained standing perfectly still and stared at him.

He arched a brow. "In this room, Beatrice, you are my property. My slave in every way. Whatever I tell you, you must do or suffer the consequences, which I promise you are not enjoyable. I am your master here."

"I have no power, then?" she whispered, uncertain if she could agree to such supplication, even for him.

He shook his head. "My dear, in some ways you have *all* the power."

"I don't understand." She wrinkled her brow.

"You can stop me at any time with just a word. You choose it, and if you say it, I must withdraw immediately, no matter how impassioned I am. Even if I am in the midst of taking you, it ends."

Beatrice's eyes widened. Here was a new twist to this idea of submission that she hadn't realized existed. What he said *did* give her ultimate power, for she had seen how involved and aroused he could become. That meant at any moment, she could withhold his pleasure from him.

With a word of her choosing. She thrust her shoulders back as he smiled at her.

"Tell me the word."

She arched her own brow. "Wicked."

He laughed, at first a chuckle and then a full belly laugh. She had never seem him as open and relaxed as this and she was mesmerized at the sight. Good God, but he was more handsome than she had thought. His laughter was almost as pleasurable as his heated touch.

"Only *you* would make *wicked* the word to say to stop me," he said as his laughter subsided. "But that is your choice and I shall abide by it. If at any time you say the word wicked, I will cease my activities immediately and you will be free to walk away from me. But anything else you say shall not stop me. Even if you tell me no."

She nodded.

"Now, strip your clothing off."

She tensed and was highly tempted to snap out the word "wicked" and stomp away, but she refrained. She had asked him to bring her here and to do this. She had berated his late wife for her refusal. It seemed her best course of action was simply to try it.

She lifted her hands to the neckline of her gown and found the first button. As she slipped it free, Gareth moved closer, his dark eyes flickering in the firelight.

"Slower, Beatrice," he breathed.

She shivered as his finger came out to trace her cheek, but she did as he asked and moved to the second button. Keeping her gaze locked with his, she freed it and tugged gently to allow the fabric to part and grant him a small glimpse of her skin beneath. He smiled and the expression was so feral and possessive that her thighs clenched around the moisture flooding her sheath.

"Again," he ordered, flicking a finger toward the next button. She freed it and the next, opening her bodice fully.

"Let me see your breasts," he whispered, his voice rough as sand. "Offer them to me."

She blushed at the frank demand, and again the word *wicked* flashed through her mind. She ignored it and shimmied the gown down her arms and her chemise. She bared her breasts and gently cupped them, lifting them from below as an offering to him.

"Pretty." He never removed his stare from the aroused peaks. "Now touch yourself. Show me your arousal."

A little whimper escaped her lips and she blushed because the sound was part denial, but equal part pleasure. It was twisted how much she liked the way he looked at her, spoke to her.

"Beatrice, I want you to answer when I tell you to do these things," he said, his pupils dilating with desire as she pinched her sensitive nipples gently. "I want you to hear yourself say yes to me."

"Y—yes," she stammered.

He shook his head. "With respect."

She narrowed her eyes, but continued to tug her nipples regardless of her outrage. "Yes, *my* lord."

His eyes fluttered shut. "Oh, I like that. Better even than *master*. That's how I want you to say it from now on."

She nodded, somehow mesmerized by the pleasure he took in what she was doing. He was giving the orders, but somehow she still had him in hand because he *needed* this from her. It was her gift, one she gave even as he took it.

"Yes, *my* lord," she whispered and was shocked how seductive her voice suddenly sounded.

"Remove the rest of the dress," he said softly. "Show me your body, because it makes me mad with wanting."

She flushed, taken aback by the compliment. How foolish and girlish it was to like that he wanted to see her body, yet warmth spread through her and settled in a steady throb between her thighs.

She pushed the dress down her body, along with her chemise. She had removed her slippers when she came into the room, so she was left in only her stockings. He growled out a low sound of pleasure.

"I'm going to buy you such beautiful, shocking underthings, Beatrice," he promised. "Shameless things to wear under proper gowns. And when you wear them, you *will* think of me and all the things I'll do to you. Do you understand?"

Her eyes fluttered shut at the image he created. She could almost picture sitting down for a proper tea with equally proper ladies, all the while wearing something utterly scandalous beneath her gown. Such a thing would make her so aware of what was awaiting her at home.

"Answer me, Beatrice," he said sharply.

"Yes," she moaned. "Yes, my lord."

"Have you ever touched yourself?" he asked.

Her eyes flew open and their gazes locked.

"You know I have," she whispered. "In the bath."

He shook his head. "I meant before you came here. Before you were mine."

She flushed, her cheeks hot as fire. "Y—yes," she finally admitted. "A few times."

"But did you ever feel release like I have given you?"

Beatrice pondered his question. She *had* furtively toyed with herself in her bed. The sensation had been lovely, but she'd never found completion until he gave it to her. Only now could she make herself orgasm.

She shook her head. "Pleasure, but never release. Not until you took me."

"You mean, I gave you your first orgasm?" he asked, eyes widening slightly and darkening with what she knew was pleasure.

"Yes, my lord," she whispered. "You taught me that pleasure."

"Very good," he growled. His eyes sparkled with wicked intent. "Now tell me, Miss Beatrice Albright, would you like one now?"

She nodded wordlessly, even though she knew the silence wouldn't be enough.

"*Tell me*," he insisted.

"I want an orgasm, my lord," she said through clenched teeth. "Please."

"Wait," he whispered. "You will, I promise you."

She shivered, for with that promise her pussy twitched in anticipation.

"Come to the table," he murmured, motioning to the place where he had taken her before. She followed him, unable to do anything but comply, when she knew he would give her such pleasure in exchange for her obedience.

She turned so that her back was facing him, like she had the first time they had sex here. Before she could bend over the table and offer herself to him, he touched her shoulder and turned her.

"Not this time," he said softly. "Lie back."

She did so. The table was surprisingly comfortable since it was padded and covered with supple leather. She relaxed, controlling her breathing and surrendering herself to watching him loom over her.

But to her surprise, he didn't take her. Instead, he grabbed one hand and lifted it above her head, snapping it into the restraint and tightening it so that she could no longer move her arm.

She jerked out of reflex and tried to free herself, but it was impossible. She stared as he repeated the action on the opposite hand.

"Gareth!" she cried out. "Stop!"

He arched a brow and smiled at her. He had told her that

he wouldn't release her unless she used that one word. And it wasn't stop.

Wicked hung on her tongue yet again, but she kept herself from using it, even though the pinning of her arms was a little frightening. Still her blood throbbed hot in her veins and she couldn't deny that just behind the fear, she felt alive with desire and passion and anticipation of what he would do to her next.

"Naughty little slave," Gareth said softly. "You don't get to tell me what to do to you. How shall I punish you, Beatrice?"

Her eyes widened further as she stared at him. "Punish?"

"Oh yes." He caught her ankle and bent her leg gently before he slipped it into the binding at the bottom of the table. She watched as he repeated that action on the opposite ankle.

Now she was truly caught, her legs spread and held open to lewdly reveal her wet and swollen sex. She was utterly at his mercy and he was saying things about punishing her.

"What will you do to me, my lord?" she asked, hating that her voice shook, but even more that the shaking wasn't only from fear.

How could she *like* this utter surrender and subjugation?

But she did. In some dark and feverish place inside of her, she loved that he robbed her of control with no apologies or remorse.

He arched a brow. "Later you will learn not to question me," he whispered. "But for now I forgive you because you are learning. What will I do to you? That is a very interesting question. You see, my dear, my intentions tonight were to bring you to orgasm over and over and over again until you were weak and begging me to come."

Beatrice couldn't help but shiver in response at the image such torment created.

Gareth chuckled. "I see you like that idea. Very nice. And later, I swear to you I will do that. You think of that while I dole out my punishment today."

"And wh—what is your punishment, lord?" Her gaze darted to the collection of lashes mounted on the wall.

Gareth followed her stare and shook his head. "Not yet, darling. You're not ready for such punishment as that. I want you to be so curious about the idea of being spanked that you come the first time I do it. No, not that. I think I shall do the opposite of my original plan."

"The opposite?"

He nodded. "Tonight I planned dozens of orgasms during hours of pleasure. But instead I think I shall doom you to only one. And you will have to wait to have it. No pleasure, no release for you, to punish you for being so naughty as to question your master."

Beatrice opened her mouth to argue, but Gareth's arched brow stopped her. If she did that, he might not let her have *any* pleasure and only torment her all night.

"If you come before I allow it," he whispered, leaning over her, "I will leave you bound here and go back to my chamber. You will have nothing and I will let the servants come and free you in the morning."

A strange titillation roared through Beatrice at the idea that strangers might see her trussed up as she was, but she turned her face so that he wouldn't see her interest.

Of course, he did. It seemed she could hide nothing from him.

"Little minx," he drawled. "I knew being watched titillated you, but not so much. Something to keep in mind for future reference, but not tonight. Unless you are very naughty. Do you understand?"

She nodded slowly.

He eased himself over her, his hot, hard body still fully clothed, while she was shamelessly naked and splayed out for his pleasure, covering her. He maneuvered until they were face to face and held her stare.

"I won't hurt you, Beatrice," he said softly, his tone pure reassurance. "You must know that and fully surrender. When you do, it will be utter pleasure for us both. I promise."

She caught her breath. In some odd way, this was him asking *her* permission. She thought of what he had said earlier, that in some way she had the higher power in this relationship, not only because she could stop it with that one word, but also because his main duty as her master was to take care of her needs. To protect her from harm and give her great pleasure. If she was obedient, she could have it. And so much more.

"I understand," she forced past dry lips and a tight throat. "And I . . . I trust you—*my* lord."

His eyes widened at that difficult admission, but then his mouth came down to cover hers and she slipped under his spell. His tongue breached her lips, filling her with heat and the taste of whiskey and mint combined.

She groaned. God, just his kiss was such pleasure. It was unfair that he could make her come undone so easily. She had never been one to surrender and yet his touch forced her. Already, she was his slave, at least with her body. She might not be ready to admit it, but she would do anything, everything for *this*.

He drew back and stared at her. "Don't come."

Before she could respond, his mouth moved down her body and he covered one aching breast with his lips. He suckled her breast slowly, languidly and finally lewdly by lapping his tongue all over the sensitive flesh.

Beatrice squirmed, but her binds kept her from moving too much. All she could do was wait and feel the tormenting pressure and power of what he was doing. The heat of his mouth moved through her bloodstream, it filled all her senses and it settled in a throbbing, pounding need between her legs. Her clit tingled and she tensed her sheath as she tried to ease the pressure.

She couldn't. With his every touch she grew more ready and wild with desire.

"You are so responsive," Gareth murmured as he slid lower, tasting her stomach, nibbling her thigh. "I cannot wait until I can make you come just by looking at you the right way."

"You could do that?" she gasped in wonder, forgetting her role as slave to his master.

He looked up as he took a position between her thighs. His dark eyes flashed with heat. "If you surrender to me fully, if you are mine in every way, I will do such things to you that when you think of them, you'll tremble."

She licked her lips, unable to stop herself. "L—like what?"

He didn't answer for a moment, busying himself instead with peeling the lips of her dripping sex open with his thumbs. He looked at her ready body and she strained for his touch even though she knew she shouldn't.

"There is so much I could do, Beatrice. One day, I will make you come in carriages, behind screens and in gardens at balls. I will pleasure you under tables at suppers. You'll find yourself thinking of my mouth and cock while you have tea with your friends. And you will ache for me and want to relieve that ache in any way you can, even if it means touching yourself in public in a ladies' salon."

Beatrice heard a moan and was shocked to realize it was her own. The images he was creating in her mind were shocking and should have been distasteful. Instead, she longed for those days. She *wanted* to be his plaything. She wanted to be so attuned to him that a look could bring her to completion. She wanted to feel owned and beautiful and alive, just like she felt right now.

"You're so close," he growled as he once again examined her wet and weeping sex. "This will be difficult for you. You cannot come, Beatrice. I don't want to punish you, but I will."

She nodded as he glanced up at her briefly. She forced herself to think of other things, but it was nearly impossible when his fingers came down to her center and he pressed one to the soaking entrance of her sheath.

Beatrice's body offered no resistance as Gareth slipped a finger deep within her. In fact, her body tugged at him, welcoming him inside her wet heat as she groaned in ecstasy. He had meant to lick her, suck her clit, but he could tell she was too close to release. The moment he pressed his mouth to her heated flesh, she would explode and he would be forced to mete out punishment.

As her master, it was his duty to help her, so he avoided her shining, hard clit and instead stroked within her with his finger. She struggled to meet his gentle thrusts, but she was bound tightly enough that she could hardly lift her hips to match his strokes. Still her sheath squeezed, holding him tightly inside and giving him so many images of feeling his cock held the same way, cradled within the protection of her warm and willing body.

He ignored the shining temptation of her clit and instead glided another finger inside her sheath. She opened for him, stretching to accept him as she cried out in pleasure. She trembled as he stroked her, but he could feel her struggling to hold back, to keep her orgasm at bay just as he had asked her to do. That fact made his desire for her swell.

Despite herself, she was making every effort to submit and from the way she thrashed her head against the soft cushioned table, she liked it. Just as he had always hoped, he had found a woman who liked the struggle for control. One who would bow to his will and take pleasure in the act of giving herself over to him.

Beatrice couldn't stop herself from moaning, crying out as Gareth invaded her with a third finger. Her sheath stretched and felt so full, yet it wasn't unpleasant. In fact, it was delicious. Especially when he curled his fingers ever so slowly. The tips rubbed the top of her sheath with increasing pleasure and then he hit upon a new spot.

Intense, explosive pleasure shot through her and she tensed, lifting against the binds with all her might as she fought to hold back the tide of pleasure his unexpected touch brought. She wanted to find release, but if she did, she was fully aware of the consequences.

But then the pressure was gone as Gareth withdrew his fingers. She watched as he lifted them to his lips and licked her juices clean. Her stomach clenched and she sighed out another moan in response.

"It's too much," he murmured.

She nodded. "Yes, *my* lord. But it was so good. So good."

"Then later I will do it again and again." He leaned over her and his eyes glittered in the firelight. "Later."

She moaned. If this was how intense all their lovemaking sessions were to be from now on, she would likely not survive. But at least she would die a happy death, in the arms of this man who could give her such pleasures like she'd never known before.

He moved away from her, crossing the room until she couldn't see him from her place on the table. She heard him moving, the swish of fabric, and then he returned, carrying some kind of slanted pillow. He set it aside and loosened her ankle restraints until she had a bit more movement in her hips.

"Lift up," he said softly.

For the first time, Beatrice didn't prickle at the order. Instead, she lifted her hips obediently and awaited whatever would come next. Gently, he slipped the pillow beneath her. She was surprised that it wasn't soft, but more formed to keep her at an angle, hips lifted ever so slightly. But with the support at her back, she didn't find the new position uncomfortable.

"Perfect," he breathed as he adjusted her ankle restraints again and stepped away. "You are offered to me like some pagan ritual."

She couldn't help but smile. This room was like a place of sacrifice, the table an altar of pleasure. She supposed that made Gareth the god and she the virgin given to appease him.

"She smiles." He chuckled as he moved a chair to the foot of the table so he could sit at the edge, right in front of her open sex and clenching bottom.

"Should I not, my lord?" she asked, fully playing along with his game now. "Would it please you more if I frowned?"

"If I asked you to, would you?" he asked, and now he seemed more serious.

She understood what he was asking. In this room, in this place, when they were making love, he needed to know that she would do as she asked and trust that there would be a reward at the end. Even if the action he demanded seemed frivolous or frightening, he *had* to feel that she would do it with no question. No hesitation.

But could she?

She nodded, almost against her will. She wanted this. And with her body, she found she did trust him.

Her reward was the quick brush of his mouth against her clenching sex. He deftly avoided her swollen clit and she could see that was a reward, not a punishment. She was so close to the edge, to disobeying his order that she not come, even if she didn't mean to do it. If he touched her there, in that aching bundle of focused pleasure, she would find her release and there would be no way to stop it.

He withdrew and his gaze snared hers again. "Trust me," he whispered.

She didn't reply, she didn't have to ask him what he meant. Gently he moved his fingers, still wet from his mouth and from her sheath, down to the apex of her body until they slipped around and suddenly he was gently caressing the rosette of her bottom. She tensed and tried to slide her hips, but the arched pillow and restraints kept her firmly in place.

"Shhh," he soothed. "I'll be gentle."

She again thought of that word that would stop this. She had only to cry out *wicked* and she could make him end this shameful new exploration of her body. She opened her mouth to say it, but found the word wouldn't come. His wet fingers gently circled the opening there, pressing the tight flesh with the right pressure and she was shocked that after the surprise of it wore off, she found that forbidden touch to be . . . *pleasurable.*

The word died on her lips and she went limp, shutting her eyes as he seduced her in yet another new way. He was infinitely gentle as he swirled his finger around and around, wetting her with the juices that now drenched her sheath and trickled onto her inner thighs.

She tensed because each time he returned his fingers to her bottom, he pressed harder, sliding into her bit by bit before letting her grow accustomed to the breach, then withdrawing. She found her breath was coming in hard, harsh pants as he dipped his finger into her sheath and then placed it back against her tight bottom.

This time, when he pressed forward, he let his finger go all the way inside to the second knuckle. She let out a cry at the twinge of pain at the invasion and squirmed a little in an effort to get away. Or perhaps get closer. She wasn't certain anymore. All the pleasure, all the new sensations, were beginning to addle her mind and she wasn't sure if she wanted to be free or to be given more.

"Let yourself relax," he murmured, his rough voice soothing. "Know I'll do nothing that isn't meant for pleasure."

She swallowed back another cry as she thought of the first time they made love. Then there had been some pain, as well, and a strangeness to being filled. And yet she had grown used to it and now she craved making love to Gareth.

She had trusted him in that moment when he promised the pain would pass. She had to do the same now.

With effort, she relaxed her body one tense muscle at a time. She focused on only the pleasure around her and let go of the pain. By the time she was finished, all that was left was a faint discomfort and strangeness.

"You are so lusciously tight," he muttered and she wasn't certain he had meant to say it out loud, which gave her a swell of triumphant power. Even tied down, a slave offering to him, she could affect him.

"I'm going to move now. Gently."

She wanted to tense, but kept herself still and relaxed, trusting him to make this experience good for her. His finger glided back and she held her breath, but to her surprise the pain she had felt had faded substantially, replaced instead by a new and intense pleasure unlike any she had ever felt. There was something about this forbidden, new act that made her sheath clench at nothingness and her clit tingle with a desire to be touched and toyed with.

He stroked within her over and over, always gentle, but never stopping. She found herself gasping for air, her hands fisting above her as she uselessly reached for more pleasure, for more intensity.

And as if he read her mind, he gave it to her. As he continued to press his finger in and out of her tight bottom, he lowered his mouth to her sheath and pressed his lips to her throbbing clit.

She couldn't withhold her cry of relief. She had been waiting for his touch there for hours, probably since they made love outside earlier in the day, and now that he did it, it was like heaven. And combined with the feel of his finger endlessly stroking in and out of her clenching bottom, she could feel herself coming to the edge of release.

She tried to stave it off, but it moved on her with steady purpose.

Finally she thrashed her head against the table and cried out, "I don't want to disobey, but I will come if you keep on like this!"

His head jerked up immediately and the rush of warmth and desire slowed. Slowly, he eased his finger from her and stood up. She lifted her head with a whimper. Had she been wrong to alert him of her impending orgasm? Did he intend to punish her for speaking out of turn?

Her fears were allayed as he reached for his wrinkled shirt and tugged it over his head. She almost sobbed as he next unfastened his trousers and kicked them away to reveal the thick, ready length of his cock at full attention against his belly.

"You have been very good," he whispered as he moved over her on the table. "And I'll give you what you seek if you can wait a little longer. Do you trust me?"

She nodded as his mouth came down and claimed hers in the same moment he slid his cock deep within her clenching, aching body. She gave a garbled groan against his rough tongue. With her hips elevated ever so slightly by the pillow beneath them, it felt like he was even deeper inside of her than ever, that he could reach new places with every stroke of his hips.

Each time he filled her, it felt like he stole more of her control. But "steal" wasn't the right word. She didn't feel taken advantage of, despite her trussed-up position and orders to call him "my lord" and do whatever he asked without question.

No, it was something better. She felt like she was safe enough to *give* him that control. To offer it and herself in a way she had always been too afraid to do.

His fingers tangled with hers and he showered her lips with hot, wet kisses that enveloped her in his world and his body and shut every other thing away. In that moment, he was everything to her. And better yet, she was everything to him.

He must have sensed her shift because he leaned around and gently kissed her earlobe before he whispered, "Come for me, Beatrice. Let go and give me your pleasure."

Her response was instant and highly intense. After withholding her pleasure for so long, now the intensity of it was multiplied. She thrashed against his body and her bounds, sobbing out relief and pleasure as her sheath was wracked with shuddering waves of release.

Although she was wrapped up in her own explosion, she was faintly aware that his hips had increased their movement, his neck strained. Just as her orgasm slowed, he let out a guttural, animal cry and filled her with his essence before he collapsed down on her sweaty naked body and held her.

She wasn't certain how long they lay like that, tangled in each other. But after some time, Gareth moved slightly and began to untie her hands, sweetly kissing the red marks where she had struggled too hard and bruised herself.

When she was free, she moved to her side and wrapped her arms around him, loving the feel of holding him when she had been unable for so long. Their breathing merged as exhaustion and sated pleasure washed over her. Her eyes grew heavy and her muscles relaxed as he smoothed his hands over her back gently.

But before she fell asleep, she made herself look at him. She smiled softly and whispered, "I think I understand, Gareth. And I want to know more. To do more. To be more."

As she slipped into sleep, she felt his lips come down on her forehead and his whisper reverberate off her skin.

"I knew you were the one, Beatrice."

And then she was gone, away to dreams filled with pleasure and warmth.

Chapter Twelve

When Beatrice walked into the dining room the next morning, Gareth got to his feet with a smile of greeting that she immediately met with a nervous one of her own. As she took a plate and began serving herself, he couldn't help but muse on how like the day was to the first morning they had spent together.

Only today there was less tension between them, less fear on Beatrice's part. Last night had changed everything between them. That much was clear.

Except, as she took her place beside him, Gareth found he was not yet satisfied. He had claimed the ultimate surrender of her body, but in truth he still knew very little about her heart and the particulars of her closely protected past. Until he had taken down that final wall between them, he was still hesitant to conclude their "test."

"You are quiet, my lord," she said as she took a big bite of her eggs.

Gareth chuckled, amused by her hearty appetite. After last night, he supposed she deserved it. And he liked that she could now be lusty in all her desires and pleasures. It meant she was growing more comfortable.

"I think last night gave us each much to think about, did it not?"

To his pleasure, her cheeks colored a fetching deep pink and her stare darted away. He found he was quite taken with the reaction. Beatrice was still innocent enough that any reference to their actions in bed or his special room continued to fluster her.

"I know I was not exactly . . ." She hesitated. "*Right* in all my behaviors."

He arched a brow. "You are still learning, Beatrice. It is my job to teach you and I intend to take great pleasure in doing so. But tell me, did you truly enjoy surrendering yourself in body to me? Could you trust me to do as I asked without hesitation?"

She set her teacup down and seemed to ponder the question for a moment. Finally, she whispered, "You and I both know that my natural inclination is not to surrender to anyone. And I admit to you that last night I had our special word, *wicked*, on my tongue more than once. But each time I held back, because I reminded myself that I *could* give you what you asked for and receive much in return."

Gareth nodded. In some ways, knowing she had wanted to make him stop and yet had trusted him enough not to do so was more satisfying than if he'd possessed her surrender from the first moment.

"Do you wish you had said it?" he asked, wanting to know that answer more than anything.

"No, Gareth," she whispered and her blue eyes held his. "I'm glad I gave you what you asked for."

He let out a breath of relief, but then shook his head. "But you haven't given me everything yet."

She drew back slightly and her eyes widened.

"What do you mean? You asked for my surrender and I gave it to you willingly. As we said, I'm still learning, but I haven't withheld anything from you."

"But you have, Beatrice."

When her brow wrinkled with concern and confusion, he continued.

"In the bedroom, yes, you are an eager student and you give me much pleasure," he said softly. "But you are not yet mine because you refuse to trust me with your past. Something made you so prickly, so driven to distance yourself from everyone else around you."

She jerked in response, as if his statement actually physically hurt her. Her hands moved to the napkin in her lap and she caught it up, twisting the fabric as she stared down at the table.

"I've asked you before and you've refused to share your past with me," he continued, reaching to trace one fingertip down the slope of her knuckle to her tangled fingers below. "And yet, you know all my secrets now."

Her gaze darted to his and he could see she had no argument. There was no doubt she recognized how painful it had been for him to share the truth about what had happened with Laurel. Certainly the death of his wife could be no less painful than any secret she had to share.

He leaned closer. "Isn't it time I hear yours?"

"I can't," she whispered, and for the first time ever Gareth heard the catch of tears in her breath.

He tilted his head and was surprised that her normally strong, unemotional expression was twisted. She trembled with pain and even fear. Until that charged moment, he hadn't fully grasped just how closely she protected her heart and her secrets.

"You gave me your body and I haven't hurt you, have I?" he asked, tilting her chin so that she looked at him.

A tear made its way down her cheek and her face colored with embarrassment. She tried to turn away, but he held her fast.

"Have I betrayed you in any way, Beatrice?" he pressed.

She hesitated, but then she shook her head. "N–no. You haven't."

"And I won't. So please trust me."

"Why is it so important to you to know what I am, who I am?" she whispered, her blue gaze meeting his briefly, then darting away like some kind of frightened animal. "Cannot it be enough that we get along as well as we do? Is there truly a need to press further?"

Gareth stroked her face lightly. "This is a lifetime we're talking about, Beatrice. I may take some things lightly, but a marriage I cannot."

"Why?" she insisted. "For most in our social sphere, it is nothing more than a business arrangement."

"My grandmother's dying wish was for me to marry again," he explained, pushing at the pain that accompanied thoughts of her. "She was the *only* person who loved me after my parents died, Beatrice. That is why I returned to Society. That is why I bore the stares and hatred of those around me. But I want more than some empty shell of a relationship. I may not require love, but I don't want the animosity I shared with Laurel at the end, either."

Beatrice was silent for a moment, then she slowly slid her face away from the cup of his hand at her chin.

"So this is about Laurel," she whispered.

When she looked down at her plate with a frown, Gareth saw that his answer troubled her. She didn't want to be compared to another woman. To have her future dictated by someone else's past.

"You and I have already talked about that," he said softly, hoping to reassure her. "I cannot erase what happened between me and my first wife—trust if I could that I would. But I have not and I will not place Laurel's memory into the bond that we share. My desire to hear your history, to understand your motivations has nothing to do with her and everything to do with *you*."

Her gaze came back to him, filled with surprise and a little hope. That vulnerability she tried to hide touched him far deeper than he had ever thought it would, for it was clear she didn't believe anyone could want her, care for her anymore.

"I *want* to know you, Beatrice," he said softly. "What happened to you to make you so cold? What forced you to turn away from everyone?"

She straightened her shoulders. Pushing the chair back, she paced away from the table to the window where she looked out over Gareth's estate. She was silent for a long time, but he didn't interrupt her. He didn't demand more. Not yet.

Finally, she sucked in a shuddering breath and began to speak. "I talked to you a little about my father."

Relief filled Gareth. Finally, he would get what he desired. "Yes. You once said you were his princess."

She nodded and the faintest hint of a smile touched her face. "He was very close to Miranda, my eldest sister, and he seemed endlessly proud of Penelope, my second eldest. Even my younger sister, Winifred, was his 'baby.' But despite there being so many of us girls, I still shared something special with him. He doted on me, giving me whatever I desired, from toys to clothing . . . even a pony one year. And I loved him with all my heart. He promised me he would always take care of me, but—"

"But?" Gareth asked softly when she broke off.

The hardness entered her eyes. "It was a lie. When he died, it was revealed that he had nothing, less than nothing. All the while he had pretended to be careful and frugal, in truth he had been gambling away our fortune without thought for what it would do to our family. My sister Miranda took up the slack, trying to keep our family from collapse, and perhaps I wasn't always kind to her. But once he was gone, nothing was the same."

"Because you no longer had money?"

She shook her head. "No. Well, yes, of course a lack of funds terrified me. My mother was hysterical and I had the pleasure of bearing witness to her endless gloomy tirades about how we would die on the streets or have to sell our bodies to save ourselves."

Gareth flinched. Beatrice would have been very young at the time, he could well imagine how difficult that must have been for her to hear and imagine.

"But it was more than that," she continued. "You said your grandmother was the only one who loved you after the death of your parents."

Gareth nodded silently.

"Well, my father was the only one who really loved me. And when he was gone, I felt so . . ." Her breath rasped harshly. "*Alone.*"

Gareth frowned. "But you weren't alone. Why didn't you bond closer to your sisters? Your mother? It seems you pushed them aside."

She turned her back to him. "There were times when I

wanted to be close to them. I saw how much my sisters cared for each other and I longed for it, but it was so difficult for me to try."

"Why?" he pressed gently.

"Losing my father hurt me deeply . . ." She folded her arms. "I began to fear losing anyone else, with an intensity that bordered on sickness. So I isolated myself, hoping I would never again feel such a void in my life."

He nodded. "It was an understandable reaction. At least for a little while."

She shrugged one slender shoulder delicately. "After a while, though, I . . . forgot how to behave differently. And there were so many things in my life that were out of my control that I felt like I still needed to protect myself."

"Out of your control?" he pressed.

She nodded, worrying her hands together. "My mother, for one. You have seen her, you've heard what people say about her. She is . . ."

Gareth watched as she struggled for a word to describe Dorthea Albright. He was surprised to recognize that Beatrice was trying to *protect* the mother she despised, despite all the ways Dorthea had sabotaged her over the years.

"She is high strung and difficult," Beatrice finally said with a blush. "Because of her own past, she reaches constantly for higher social ground, but nothing is good enough for her. And when my elder sisters married an earl and a duke respectively, that only encouraged her madness. She fed me constant tirades about how I was better than everyone, how I deserved

as much as my sisters had married. In the beginning, I believed her."

"But not anymore?" Gareth whispered, longing to comfort
her, but realizing it was not the course of action to take. Her
confession was a difficult one, if he touched her she would
construe it as pity and shut him out.

She looked at him briefly. "I don't know. So much has
changed. In the beginning, my looks and my ties to important families in my two brothers-in-law gave me some advantage in Society. There were suitors. There were even men I—I
liked."

Gareth stiffened, unexpected and irrational jealousy filling him at the idea that she had been attracted to men who
courted her. "Why did you not marry one of them?"

"My mother kept railing on me to reach for better. At the
time, it seemed she was correct, I had so many choices. And
in truth, I feared the kind of closeness that a marriage would
bring. In the end, I pushed any man I liked away and watched
each marry other girls, one by one."

She stiffened and he could see how much that had hurt her
and filled her with regrets.

"The ones I didn't like, I came to resent just as much for
their false words and lack of polish. As the Seasons went on,
there were fewer and fewer who turned their eyes toward me.
Soon people were talking, avoiding me because of my behavior, because of my mother."

"It must have been difficult for you," he said softly.

She nodded. "But I fought the pain and instead my bitterness increased, spreading to every part of me until anything deeper or kinder was killed, poisoned and smothered. And I became . . . a *shrew* is what they call me, isn't it? A bitch."

She faced him and her cheeks were aflame with embarrassment that she had revealed so much. Her chin was lifted high, though, a challenge for him to mock her or try to knock her down now that he had the ammunition to do so.

Instead, he reached out and finally did what he had longed to do since she began speaking. He took her hand. She gasped and watched as he lifted it and pressed a soft, sensual kiss to her knuckles before he drew her forward a few steps. Not quite in his arms, but close enough that he could feel her warmth and smell her perfume.

"I don't see a shrew, Beatrice," he murmured. "I only see *you*. *My* Beatrice. And I hope . . ." He hesitated. "I hope my future bride."

Her lips parted and she drew back just a fraction to look up at him in awe and surprise. "You are asking me——"

His nod cut her off. "Yes. I think we've passed all the tests we came here to perform, don't you? We agreed that if we were compatible, we would wed. Do you still want that?"

Beatrice swallowed hard enough that he saw her delicate throat work with the action. Her pale skin was even lighter as she looked up at him. He found himself holding his breath as he awaited her response. The moment she said yes, he was packing her into his carriage and hauling her to Gretna Green to make their union legal.

But before her bloodless lips could give her answer, the

door behind them opened. Gareth spun on the intruder with murder in his eyes and found it was the footman, Hodges, who had intruded upon his privacy and what was swiftly becoming the longest moment of his life.

He glared at the servant and was briefly surprised when the man returned the expression evenly before his face became impassive.

"What is it, Hodges?" he snapped out. "I'm a bit busy here."

"I'm sorry, sir, but you have guests," the servant said with a sniff.

"Guests?" Gareth barked. "I'm not expecting anyone. They can bloody well wait."

The footman arched a brow. "They have made it clear that they will not wait, my lord. In fact, they have threatened to storm the house and search for you if you do not see to them immediately."

That caught Gareth's attention and he released Beatrice's hand to turn fully toward the door. "What the bloody hell? Who are they?"

"The Earl and Countess of Rothschild, my lord," the servant said benignly.

Behind him, Beatrice made a loud sound of distress and took a long step forward. "M—my sister and her husband?"

"Indeed," the footman said with a brief glance in her direction. "What shall I do?"

Gareth gave Beatrice a side glance. She looked utterly irritated and slightly terrified, but it seemed there was nothing to be done about it. If the Lord and Lady Roths-child were here, unannounced and threatening to search his home, there was no doubt they suspected Beatrice was in residence.

He shrugged. "Show the earl and his wife in," Gareth said with a forced smile. "They shall no doubt provide the morning entertainment."

The one thing that had always been said about Ethan Hamon, Earl of Rothschild, was that he dominated any room. And although Beatrice had never connected with her eldest sister's husband, she had always respected his ability to make any other man in a chamber fade.

When he entered the breakfast room, Gareth didn't fade. Even as the earl stepped forward with a menacing glare, Gareth didn't so much as blink, let alone step down. If anything, he seemed *bored* by it all and Beatrice just barely reigned in an urge to laugh at his audacity.

"Good God!" her sister, Miranda said as she released her husband's arm and rushed forward.

To Beatrice's surprise, her sister enveloped her in the warmest, hardest hug she had ever felt. Miranda was trembling as she clung to her. Finally, her sister stepped back and her ashen-gray face was long and filled with censure.

"I am not sure if I should be thrilled to find you unharmed or furious to see that you have gone so far, Beatrice."

All the brief warmth and closeness Beatrice had felt in Miranda's arms faded in an instant.

"Try both," she said with a frown. "Then you won't have to choose."

Miranda let out her breath in a put-upon sigh and returned to her husband's side. Together they glared at Beatrice and Gareth, a united front in their judgments and disappointments.

"I think you had best explain yourself, Highcroft," Ethan said as he held glares with Gareth.

"Why don't you talk to me?" Beatrice snapped, drawing her brother-in-law's attention to her. "Instead of him? *I'm* the one you came here to find."

"But *he* is the one who dragged you here and utterly ruined you," Miranda cried, her blue gaze bright with the fire of her upset. "How dare you, sir?"

Beatrice shook her head. "He brought me here at *my* request."

She shot Gareth a side glance and found that he was simply watching her with a bemused smile on his face, as if this truly was an entertainment to him. But beneath that calm exterior she could see the tension in his shoulders, the readiness to defend her if it came to that.

But for now, he was allowing her to handle the situation as she saw fit. She smiled at him in response and the connection they shared practically glowed.

Miranda exchanged a worried look with her husband before she speared Beatrice with a glare. "What do you mean he brought you here at your request? What is going on, Beatrice?"

"I'm going to marry him," she said softly.

At that, the chamber erupted in her sister and brother-in-law's exclamations of dismay and refusal. Beatrice folded her arms and stepped closer to Gareth. She smiled when she felt his fingers brush the small of her back in reassurance. She had spent so many years loathe to depend on anyone, and yet now she reveled in his support and quiet strength.

Ethan interrupted that sweet moment by lunging forward and grasping Gareth's collar with both fists.

"I don't think so, mate," he growled. "Not when you might have killed your first wife."

Beatrice let out a gasp of outrage and grabbed for one of Ethan's arms, while Miranda grasped the other. Both women tugged, but the two men remained locked.

"How dare you!" Beatrice panted as she pulled uselessly to force Ethan to release Gareth. "You know nothing about him or his past. Stop it! Release him at once."

"Miranda," Ethan said without looking at his wife. No, he kept his gaze locked firmly on Gareth even as he slowly released him. "Take your sister for a walk in the garden. You two have much to talk about and I want a moment with Lord Highcroft, here."

"No," Beatrice cried out, wedging herself between the men now that a space had been created. "I won't allow you to—"

"Beatrice," Gareth said quietly but firmly from behind her.

Slowly, she turned and looked at him. He held her gaze and she could see the steel in his stare. The order about to come.

And she saw in that moment that she would not refuse him. Even if she wanted to.

"Go with your sister."

Her breath left her lungs in a long sigh. "But what if he—" she whispered.

He shook his head. "Beatrice."

Biting her lip, Beatrice nodded and quietly turned toward Miranda. She glared at Ethan as she made for her sister and only paused for one look at Gareth before she shut the door behind her and left the two men alone.

While she prayed it wouldn't be the last time she saw Gareth.

Chapter Thirteen

$\mathcal{M}$iranda was curiously silent as the two of them made their way through the estate and out into the garden, but Beatrice felt her sister's stare on her with every step. That intense scrutiny made Beatrice squirm and finally she turned on Miranda with her hands on her hips.

"Go ahead. Say whatever it is you want to say to me. Tell me what a horror I am and a disappointment and anything else. I don't care."

But even as she said the words, she realized they were a lie. She *did* care, even if she never said that out loud. No matter how little she deserved it, in her heart, Beatrice wished her sister accepted her the way she did Penelope or Winifred.

"Actually, I wasn't going to say any of those things," Miranda said softly. "I have merely been marveling at how easily you followed Lord Highcroft's request—rather, *command*—that you leave him alone with Ethan. However did he manage to garner such obedience from you?"

Beatrice blushed and moved away from her sister in a few long strides. There was no way she was going to explain to Miranda about the games of dominance and surrender she had come to enjoy.

But it seemed she didn't have to explain anything. Her sister pursed her lips and sat down hard on the nearest bench.

"Ah, I see." Miranda let out a sigh. "Well, I suppose it *is* to be expected considering the history of our family."

A sting worked through Beatrice at her sister's words.

"You mean how I've always been different from you all?" Beatrice asked even as she sank down beside her sister. Suddenly she was very tired of all of this. She couldn't even manage a sharp tone as she sighed. "How I've always been a disappointment and my ruination is proof of it?"

Miranda turned toward her and for the first time in a long time, her sister was smiling. She covered her mouth, but not before a giggle escaped her lips.

"Good Lord, are you that naïve? Heavens, Beatrice. *All* of the girls in our family have been ruined in one way or another."

"What are you talking about?"

Miranda shrugged. "I entered into an affair with Ethan long before we wed. And Penelope did Lord knows what with Jeremy, all while carrying on about the sins of the *ton*."

Beatrice leaned back, shocked speechless. There had always

been faint rumors about her family, of course, but she'd never believed them. Miranda and Penelope were so settled and sure and . . . *perfect*, she'd never thought they could stray or demand passion or make a scene.

She folded her arms, uncomfortable with the realization of how blind she had apparently been.

"How did you find me?" she asked, desperate to change the subject since she didn't know what to say in the face of Miranda's confession.

Miranda sighed. "You didn't make it easy for us, that is certain. When Mama showed up unannounced at Penelope and Jeremy's country party, saying she had received her invitation, we were suspicious. Jeremy and Ethan began discreetly inquiring after where you might be. And since your friend you claimed to be retreating with was actually still in London and knew nothing of your whereabouts, it was clear you were off doing something careless."

Beatrice pursed her lips. She wasn't sure she considered the time she'd spent here as "careless."

"I was merely protecting my future," she retorted.

Miranda arched a brow. "Is that what you call it? At any rate, a few people had seen you with Lord Highcroft and . . ."

"Ah." Beatrice snapped, annoyed by her sister's dismissiveness. "But Penelope and Jeremy couldn't be bothered to pursue me. Written me off, have they?"

Miranda looked at her in surprise, but then her expression softened. "No, to the contrary. Jeremy wished to ride here himself, probably to flog Highcroft within an inch of his life, but we didn't want to raise suspicion from the rest of their party, especially since . . ."

Her sister faded off, looking out across the garden with a troubled frown.

"Since?" Beatrice asked, leaning closer.

"Well, er, you were not the only one discovering pleasure, it seems," Miranda said softly. "Our sweet Winifred has apparently been much educated over the years by a rather large hidden collection of naughty books and decided to pursue her own chance at happiness. She was caught in a rather bad position with the second son of the Viscount Valeron. They are to be married as soon as we can fetch you home. That was the excuse we gave to depart to find you."

Beatrice stared at her sister, completely taken aback by the news she had just been given. "*Winifred* and Milo Valeron?"

"Indeed." Miranda shrugged.

Beatrice blinked. Milo Valeron was well known for his lusty appetites. She could scarcely imagine her quiet younger sister catching his eye. But perhaps she didn't know Winifred as well as she thought.

"And they are to be married?" she repeated.

Miranda nodded with a look of resignation to the idea. "She seems very happy, as does the future groom. And since, as I explained, neither Penelope nor I have much room to disapprove, we are determined to be happy for her. I hope you will be, too. She much fears your reaction."

Beatrice flinched as she thought of all the ways she had hurt her sensitive younger sister. Although she had never been exactly proud of herself, this was the first time she truly felt guilt over her actions.

"I have been hateful toward her," she whispered, her gaze coming up to Miranda.

Miranda nodded, more solemn than ever. "That was part of why Ethan and I took her away, in the hopes that without your influence, she might flower. It seems we were more correct than we hoped."

Beatrice nodded. She was trying to picture a passionate Winifred, but couldn't exactly do it. Finally, she shrugged. "Yes."

"Will you be able to wish her well?" her sister asked.

Beatrice considered it. When they were very young, she and Winifred had been close. Their nearness in age had formed a bond between them that she had shattered after their father's death. Perhaps now . . . perhaps she could repair it.

"Yes," she whispered. "When I see her, I will wish her well and apologize to her about what I did."

Miranda drew back as if surprised, but then she smiled. "Good. I'm certain that will mean a great deal to her."

"But can you wish *me* well, sister?" Beatrice asked. "Can you give me the same support that you give Winifred, even though you do not have the same depth of feeling toward me?"

Miranda grasped her hands, her expression softening and growing sad. "Is that what you think? That I have less feeling toward you than I do our other sisters?"

Beatrice lifted her chin with defiance even as her heart

swelled with sadness. They had never spoken of these things aloud before. Finally, she nodded slightly.

"It is no secret that you do not . . . *like* me. And perhaps that is partly of my own design."

"I cannot say that you haven't occasionally been difficult to handle. But dearest, my objections to your union with Lord Highcroft have nothing to do with my depth of feeling for you." Miranda squeezed her fingers lightly. "On the contrary, they are based in my deepest fear that he might hurt you and I wouldn't be able to protect you. You have heard the rumors about him, about what happened to his wife. What if they are true?"

Beatrice withdrew her hands from her sister's, still uncomfortable with such a gesture.

"They aren't," she said with all the conviction she felt in her heart.

"But—"

Beatrice got to her feet and paced away, keeping her back to her sister. "I said *no*. Nothing that has been said about Gareth is true."

"How do you know?" Miranda pressed.

Beatrice squeezed her eyes shut. "He told me the truth about what happened to Laurel." Slowly she faced her sister. "Even if he hadn't . . . a woman knows in her heart."

Miranda stared at her for a long, charged moment. Beatrice could see that her sister wanted to say more, wanted to ask more, perhaps even wanted to argue more, but when she spoke it was to do none of those things.

"I suppose you are right. A woman *does* know." Miranda shrugged. "Certainly there was much said about both Ethan and Jeremy before they joined our family. They didn't even trust each other at first. But now they are as close as any blood brothers could be. Nothing that was said about them was really true at the heart of them."

Beatrice nodded as she found herself briefly wondering if Gareth would ever fit into her family as well. If he would even want to. Their marriage might have passion, but neither of them had promised the other the soul connection that her sisters seemed to have with their husbands. Secretly, she had always envied that.

She shook away the thoughts.

"I know better than anyone that the *ton* can be unkind," she said softly. "They talk and pick and judge. But I know the truth, so please trust that Gareth may be many things, but a murderer is not one of them."

Her sister was slow to nod and Beatrice could see that Miranda would have to hear Ethan's word on the subject before she was fully comfortable with Gareth and his offer to wed Beatrice.

Still, her sister's expression was softer than it had been when they came to the garden.

"I will say one thing, you do look happy." Miranda tilted her head slightly. "Happier than I have seen you in a long time."

Beatrice stared at her sister as her thoughts moved to her family in the days before her father's death. Until today, she had never spoken to anyone about her grief or the reasons for her self-exile.

Now she shook her head and surprised herself by whispering, "You don't think you and Penelope and Winifred were the only ones who lost a father, do you? Who lost everything?"

Miranda took a long step forward. "Of course not. I know you were hurt as badly as any of us. And in part, I understood that you lashed out in your pain. I only wish I could have helped you more. Then and now."

Beatrice smiled at her sister, the first real smile they had shared in so many years that she could scarcely recall the last time.

"I wouldn't have let you," she admitted.

Miranda laughed softly. "But maybe you will now?"

Beatrice nodded. "Yes. Perhaps."

Then she shook her head. This was enough confession and bonding for one afternoon.

"Come, let us return before the men kill each other."

Her sister seemed to understand her discomfort, for she merely nodded and let Beatrice lead her to the house. But as they went inside together, Beatrice sighed. For the first time in a long time, she felt like she was Miranda's sister again. And she liked it more than she had ever hoped she would.

Gareth folded his arms as he watched the Earl of Rothschild pace the chamber, his anger clear in every part of him. The other man was menacing, there was no denying it. He was big and muscular and looked like he could throw a solid punch.

But Gareth wasn't one to be easily intimidated.

Rothschild turned on him with a pointed glare. "At what point do you intend to explain yourself, Highcroft?"

Gareth shrugged. "What is there to explain? I think we both know what has happened between Beatrice and I. And I have offered her marriage, she has accepted."

Ethan took a long step toward him. "You bastard. Of course she accepted, she is ruined. She is—"

Gareth arched a brow. "It is no less than what rumor states happened between you and *your* wife not so very long ago. At least I proposed to Beatrice in the privacy of my home, not in the middle of a ball in front of everyone."

Rothschild's eye twitched and his nostrils flared. Yes, Gareth could definitely see why he was so revered and even feared by some.

"I do appreciate this display of protectiveness," Gareth drawled. "I simply wonder where it was when Beatrice actually needed it."

He had known the reaction such a statement would elicit when he said it, but at the moment he didn't care. Gareth found he actually wanted the challenge of Ethan Hamon's anger. He wanted to make Beatrice's family question their actions and see that he would defend her honor . . . even from them.

So when Ethan launched across the room with a growl, fists raised, Gareth was ready. He blocked the first punch and the men ended up grappling, grasping for fistfuls of jacket and staggering about the room with their glares locked and each muttering epitaphs about the other.

"Stop it!"

Both men released each other instantly as Beatrice flew into the room with Miranda close at her heels. As Miranda caught her husband's arm and drew him away, Beatrice glared at her brother-in-law with a look that had likely scarred many a man before.

"How *dare* you?" Beatrice huffed.

Ethan shook his head as if he couldn't believe she took Gareth's side over his. "We are here for *your* protection!"

"I don't want your protection," Beatrice cried out in return. "Not from him. You don't know a damn thing about this situation."

"I know you shouldn't stay here, you shouldn't be here!" Ethan said with an exasperated exhalation of breath. "For God's sake, Miranda, say something."

Instead, Beatrice's sister reached up and caressed her husband's cheek. Gareth watched in utter fascination as the growling, furious man who had attacked him was transformed as his gaze fell to his wife. They held stares for a long, charged moment where a thousand unspoken words moved between them with the kind of ease one only had with the one they loved.

Gareth glanced down and saw that Beatrice was at rapt attention, as well. As if she felt his stare, she glanced at him, then looked away with a blush. That kind of connection wasn't one they had found yet, nor even pledged.

And in the face of it, their physical bond paled slightly.

"Come away, Ethan," Miranda said softly. "We are all

filled with much high emotion with everything that has transpired during the last few days. I know your only wish is to protect my sisters, and I love you for that more than you shall ever know, but this is not a decision to be made in this moment."

Ethan stared at her, then slid his gaze back to Gareth slowly. "We shall take her with us to the inn tonight."

Gareth arched a brow in challenge before he looked at Beatrice. "Is that what *you* desire?"

Her eyes were wide and her hands came to her hips. "Absolutely not. You cannot come marching in here and tell me what to do, Ethan Hamon! I am staying here and that is final."

"Beatrice——" Ethan snapped.

Before the sister and brother-in-law could come to blows, Gareth stepped forward.

"I understand your desire to protect your wife's sister, Lord Rothschild," he said smoothly, presenting Ethan with the respect he had thus far withheld. "You aren't certain of me, my past or even my intentions, so you do not wish to leave her here, yet she refuses to leave with you. We are at an impasse, so I propose that you two forego the inn and stay at my estate. That way Beatrice will not feel she has been dragged away against her will and you two won't be left in the uncomfortable position of surrendering her to my care."

No one in the room responded. Miranda Hamon simply stared at him, appraising and beautiful, though he felt her beauty paled in comparison to Beatrice. Ethan watched Beatrice, and Beatrice glared in return.

Finally Gareth sighed. "Would that be acceptable to all parties?"

It was Miranda who replied. "Yes. I think that is a very good suggestion, Lord Highcroft. And if we stay here, it will also allow my husband and me to get to know you better." She touched Ethan's arm. "We certainly understand that not all gossip is true, don't we, dear?"

Ethan finally let his gaze return to Gareth. "Yes, I suppose we do, after all."

"Then Lord Highcroft is affording us a very fair chance to see him here and judge his character for ourselves."

After a long moment, Ethan nodded. "Yes. Very well, we shall stay."

It seemed like everyone in the room exhaled in relief at the same moment and Gareth smiled. "Very good. I shall arrange for my man to go to the village and deliver your things here straightaway."

But as Gareth left the room to find a servant, he couldn't help but sigh. In the midst of the most pleasurable few days of his life, suddenly everything was far more complicated. And it seemed it was destined to remain that way until he had proven the rumors about him wrong.

Chapter Fourteen

Just as Gareth had suspected they would be, the past few hours had been some of the most uncomfortable in his life. By the time Lord and Lady Rothschild were settled and their items brought from the inn, it had been close to suppertime. The meal had been a tense one, to say the least. Every word he said was analyzed and every look meaningful.

While Miranda Hamon seemed to be willing to reserve judgment about him for her sister's sake, her husband still retained an air of outright distrust.

Not that Gareth blamed the earl. There was much to be wary of when it came to Gareth's past. But he had spent so long outside the reaches of Society, avoiding that kind of censure that he found in the man's judging stare. It was very grating to be forced to endure it now.

Any other night he would have given himself over to the pleasure of a woman to relieve the strain, but his current situation seemed to preclude that option.

With her sister and brother-in-law in the house, surely Beatrice was off-limits. Although Gareth wasn't afraid of Ethan Hamon, he did not want to come to blows with the earl, either. Such a thing would not make earning his trust any easier. Nor did Gareth wish to damage the already fragile bond between Beatrice and her sister. Whether she admitted it or not, Beatrice wanted the approval of her family. And if they had that, it would make a marriage between them far more accepted by Society.

Gareth could, of course, arrange to meet with another woman. He had several in the area whom he called upon from time to time to slake his needs in the way he liked. Women who calmly gave themselves to him without hesitation, but without much enthusiasm, either.

Unlike Beatrice. And he found, in a very troubling moment of self-reflection, that he did not wish to satisfy his desire with anyone but her.

Trying to ignore that thought, he pushed his chamber door open and entered the dimly lit room. He rubbed his pounding temples as he pushed the door shut behind him.

"Good evening, *my* lord."

Gareth's gaze jerked up. Across the chamber, standing in the doorway between his dressing room and his bedroom, was Beatrice. She was wrapped in a silken robe, her blond hair down around her shoulders in a cloud.

"B—Beatrice?" he stammered in surprise as he moved toward her. "What are you doing here?"

A tiny smile quirked up the corner of her lip, but he also saw pure defiance sparkle in her stare. It was utterly arousing to see that tart expression there and know that Beatrice might have surrendered herself completely to him, but not to anyone else.

She slipped her hands down the apex of her body and slowly loosened the knot at her waist. With a shake of her golden locks, she let her robe fall away.

She was utterly, delectably naked beneath, rosy red nipples already at attention. Her smile widened.

"No one tells me what to do," she whispered. "Except you. *My* lord."

Gareth crossed the room so fast that it seemed to surprise Beatrice, for she laughed nervously at his ardor. But when his arms came around her, her smile faded and she made no move to resist. In fact, her body molded to his and her mouth opened as he pressed his lips to hers. As he breathed her in, she let out a needy, passionate growl of pure pleasure.

Gareth lifted her from her feet. Her legs locked around his waist as he carried her across the room to his bed. She didn't let go, even as he laid her back across the soft coverlet and she didn't break the hot, wet kiss.

She was as hungry for him as he was for her. He could tell by the way she tore at his clothes, raking her nails across his skin as they tossed layer after layer aside. And all the while her hips kept grinding against his, rubbing his cock through

the rapidly tightening confines of his trousers with a frustrat-
ingly perfect rhythm.

"How did you do this to me?" she gasped as their fingers
tangled at his waistband.

Together they tugged at his belt and struggled with the
fastenings of his pant waist. When his trousers finally hit the
floor and he kicked them away, she drew back a fraction and
looked at him from head to toe. He moaned as she licked her
lips with a feral possessiveness that made his cock so hard it
actually ached.

"What did I do?" he asked her as he positioned himself over
her and braced his arms on either side of her head. But he
didn't enter her, not yet.

"You have made me a wanton, so attuned and in longing
to your body that I would beg for it. I would do anything you
asked for it." She shook her head in wonderment. "How did
you do that?"

He smiled. "I only awoke what you are, Beatrice. *Who* you
are."

Slowly, he thrust forward. His cock breached her wet body
with no resistance and he shuddered as her sheath clung to
him as he moved within her. Her body was like a hot, wet
glove, holding him so tight that he could easily explode like
a green boy.

"And what and who you are," he panted, "is *mine*."

She nodded. "I'm yours."

Her words broke off on a cry as he thrust back and then

pounded into her even harder than before. Her thighs tightened around his waist and she lifted into the harsh thrust.

"And whatever else you are, in my bed, you submit to my every desire and you trust that I will take care of you," he whispered.

She nodded silently, her face twisted in a mask of pure ecstasy and he pulled back so his cock was almost entirely out of her body. When she gave a low whimper of longing, he shook his head.

"Say the words, Beatrice."

"In your bed, in your arms, *you* are the master," she admitted. "And I know you will withhold release and also make me come all with my ultimate pleasure in mind."

He drew back and straightened her long, smooth legs, draping her knees over his shoulders. And then he took her. There was no doubt in the taking. Their coupling was fast and hard and infinitely animal. He drove into her with no mercy, driving her toward pleasure and desire and the future with every arch of his hips.

She thrashed helplessly, lifting her hips into his every thrust and crying out as she was filled by him. Her fingers fisted in the bedsheets, her head rocked back and forth. He could feel her getting so close to pleasure, but she never quite found it.

Because she needed his permission.

Finally, after all the years of searching, after all the pain of

Laurel's repulsion over what he was and what he needed . . . here, lying beneath him, accepting his cock, was the perfect woman for him.

One who had surrendered herself to him in every way, despite how terrifying a prospect that was to her.

"Come for me, Beatrice," he murmured, granting her the gift she had earned with her trust and submission.

There was no doubt she had been on the edge for a long time, because her orgasm was the most intense he had seen her experience. Her screams filled the air, so loud that he began to wonder if she might bring the house down. Her body thrashed and trembled and it seemed to go on forever as he continued to take her and guide her through the pleasure, toward the final release.

Finally, she went limp beneath him, completed satiated. He hadn't found his release yet, but still he withdrew from her trembling sheath and took a place beside her, his hard cock, still wet with her essence, resting against her thigh.

Her eyes came open and she looked at him.

"I don't understand," she whispered as she glanced down. "You didn't . . ."

"Not yet," he said, brushing back tangled locks from her face. "Today I asked you a question, but before you could reply we were interrupted by the arrival of your sister and her husband."

She nodded and he noted that her legs still trembled from her orgasm. "Yes."

"Do you have an answer for me?"

She sat up a fraction. "I told Ethan and Miranda that I would marry you. You heard me say it."

A shrug was his reply. "You said it, but it was as much to upset them as it was any other reason."

Her lips pursed with displeasure for a brief moment, but then she smiled. "I suppose there was some element of that to my saying it."

"I want an answer that is only for me," he said. "I want to know if you will marry me."

"Are you certain you still want to wed even after Ethan and Miranda's highhandedness?" she whispered and now she pressed a hand to his chest.

He nodded.

She drew in a deep breath. "Yes. I want to marry you."

The relief that made itself known in every part of Gareth's mind and soul was not something he had expected when he made this bargain. But then, so much about Beatrice had been a delightful surprise.

And now he had a lifetime to discover even more about her. They were certainly compatible in bed and he liked her, despite of . . . or perhaps *because of* how prickly she could be. She was a challenge and he liked that about her.

"You are staring," she whispered. "Did you want something more from me?"

He grinned. "Yes, something more."

Her eyes lit up as her gaze flitted down to his still-hard cock. Then she leaned over and kissed him, hot and wet and filled with surrender and possession and desire.

"What can I do for you, *my* lord?" she whispered, her blue eyes lifting as she met his gaze.

He shivered with pleasure at all the wonderful images her question created. It was like he was a child brought to a sweet shop and told he could have anything and everything he desired. How could he choose with such delicacy spread out before him?

He smiled. "There are so many answers to your question, my dear, I can scarcely pick just one."

A light laugh unlike any he'd ever heard from her escaped her lips and made him look at her more closely.

"Why pick *one* then?" she said, batting her eyes in a most fetching way.

Leaning down, he caught her cheeks and dragged her in for a hot, hard kiss. She melted into him, arching her hips against his and nearly unmanning him in the process.

With much difficulty, he pulled away and stared down at her. "I do have one desire."

"Name it."

He met her gaze evenly. "I would like to claim the one last virgin place in your body."

Her eyes widened with confusion and a tinge of worry.

"Wha—"

Gareth reached out and gently parted the globes of her bottom. Pressing his fingers against the tight hole there, he held her stare without so much as blinking.

Beatrice swallowed hard, all playfully sensual thoughts fleeing her mind. She recalled the last time he had touched her like he was touching her now. Just his finger had brought her so much pleasure, but also pain, and his cock was so much larger. She couldn't imagine him fitting it into the shallow channel he wished to breach.

"Is—is that possible?" she asked.

He leaned forward and placed a brief kiss to the tip of her nose. "I would not suggest it if it weren't."

Beatrice stared, as taken aback by the sweetness of his kiss as she was by the shock of his suggestion. But finally, she nodded. It was time for the final surrender.

"Gareth, I have given over my pleasure to you. In all ways, you are the master of it. And if this is what you want and what you believe I need, then . . ."

She didn't finish, but instead rolled to her stomach and lifted her backside up in mute offering.

Gareth let out a lewd curse and Beatrice couldn't help but smile. He hadn't expected such bold surrender, even if he wanted it. Surprising him was a pleasure.

He moved behind her slowly, parting her legs to kneel between them on the bed behind her. Beatrice put her face into the pillows, readying herself for pain, praying for pleasure to balance it.

But Gareth didn't simply take. His warm hands cupped her bottom, gently massaging the flesh there, reverently stroking her as if he were worshipping a goddess.

She relaxed at the pleasurable touch, sighing into the pillows as the tension bled from her muscles. He leaned over her to open a drawer in the table beside his bed. She didn't lift her head to see what he retrieved, but when he moved back over her and returned his hands to her skin, she gasped when a warm liquid touched her.

Lifting her head, she looked over her shoulder. Gareth loomed over her, his hard cock tight to his stomach and his big hands coated in some kind of wet, oily substance.

"What is that?" she whispered.

"Only olive oil," he murmured as he glided his hands back to her bottom. "It will help."

She nodded, mesmerized as she watched his oily hands caress her skin. Without any friction to hinder his touch, it was a whole new experience. It was like she was underwater, and yet she was so much more sensitive to the warmth of his skin, the brush of his fingers.

"Gareth," she choked out, clutching the pillow above her with gripping fingers.

He didn't answer, but instead parted her bottom again and slipped his slick fingers between the globes. With the added lubrication, her channel offered nothing to stop him and his finger glided inside of her without any trouble or the pain she had experienced before.

The fullness of his fingers was different in this forbidden place than it was when he took her pussy. Because she was untried, the sensations were far more raw and her reactions were less controlled. She fisted her hands against the pillow and cried out softly.

"You are so tight around me," he groaned, the tension clear

in his voice. "And so hot, Beatrice. So hot. I can't wait to feel you around my cock."

"I want that, *my* lord," she said, slipping easily into her role as his supplicant. "I want to feel you within me. Please."

He chuckled. "Such a good little wanton. But I must ready you. Relax and let me pleasure you."

She nodded with only a brief glance at him over her shoulder. And then, perhaps for the first time, she truly gave herself over to him without question, without worry. She forgot all her fears and trusted him to save her, to take her, to make her whole with his body.

He didn't disappoint. He stroked one finger in and out, lubricating her tight channel with the oil he had spread over his fingers. When she was moaning and thrusting back in time, he added a second digit. She felt him stretching her ever so slowly, widening her in readiness for his much bigger erection.

Then a third finger joined. By this time, she was thrashing against the pillow, lifting her hips helplessly as her empty pussy clenched and wept for him.

"Touch yourself, Beatrice," he said, his tone harsh in the quiet room. "And you have my permission to come. Come for me, over and over."

Greedy, Beatrice slid shaking fingers between her legs. When she cupped the mound there, she found she was already wet, ready to be taken. But Gareth would not return to her clenching body tonight. No, he was giving her a new experience.

She yelped in pleasure as she stroked her fingers over herself. With Gareth's permission to find pleasure as often as she liked ringing in her ears, she brought herself to swift relief within a few hard strokes.

"Gareth!" she cried out as waves of pleasure washed over her. She continued to stroke herself as she came, overcome by the never-ending stretch of his fingers and the fluttering brush of her own. She felt full and alive and so aware of her own desire that it seemed like her world revolved around it.

Just as her first orgasm faded, she felt Gareth shift. He pressed the head of his cock to the rosette of her bottom and then rested there, his breath coming hard and hot behind her.

She was weak with release, but Beatrice made herself look at him. "It feels so good," she moaned.

"And it will be better," he promised, his dark eyes glittering in the firelight. "Let me take you. Relax and let the pain wash away and be replaced by a sensation that will make your pleasure all the better."

She nodded. "Yes."

With her permission given, Gareth pressed forward. At first he was slow, letting her body relax around him, breaching her with steady, even pressure. He felt Beatrice clench her muscles just the slightest bit and knew she was feeling the pain of the joining, even though he had readied her and lubricated her channel and his member.

"Relax," he soothed. "Touch your clit. Feel the pleasure with the pain."

She hesitated for a moment and he almost thought she would pull away, but instead her trembling fingers moved between her legs. She worked herself with purpose, rubbing her clit, gently fingering herself and with every stroke her bottom relaxed, letting him inch forward bit by bit until he filled her completely.

"God," he moaned, "You feel so good, sweetling. So tight around me."

She didn't respond, but instead cried out as a second orgasm moved through her. Gareth let his head flop back. Her sheath fluttered and trembled, he felt it through the thin separation between the two channels and it massaged his cock in a most pleasurable way.

Beatrice continued to writhe beneath him and Gareth drew back ever-so-gently and then thrust forward. Her cries intensified, but she didn't tense and he realized that the thrust had only made her orgasm more powerful. Her body had accepted what he desired.

He thrust again, still gentle, but deeper, taking and taking, loving how she clenched against him, how she continued to pleasure herself as she heaved out heavy breaths and moans. She came a third time and just as the tremors of that release faded, a fourth.

Beatrice could hardly breathe, the pleasure was so intense. She was a slave to it now, a slave to the burning heat in one entrance and the shuddering thrill of the other. She wanted more, she wanted Gareth, she wanted this forever.

"I'm yours," she cried out, her hips slamming back against his thrusts and demanding he take her harder. "I'm yours."

Her admission seemed to drive him over the edge. He let out an animal cry unlike anything she'd ever heard before. His thrusts, which had been gentle, turned harsh, punishing, and suddenly she felt the ripple of his release fill her as he flopped over her to cover her body with his.

They lay like that for some time and finally he sat up and gently withdrew from her sore, used bottom.

"I'm sorry," he gasped as he reached for a cloth beside the bed and cleaned her gently. "I should not have lost control. It was ungentlemanly of me."

She smiled as she rolled over beneath him and looked up at him. Catching his cheeks, she drew him closer.

"I've *never* mistaken you for a gentleman, Gareth," she whispered.

A swift, sensual grin was her reward and she basked in the warmth of his amused regard. Then he pushed a bit of her hair away.

"Still, I could have prepared you. I could have controlled myself," he said softly.

She shrugged. "If we are to be married, then it seems we will *each* have to trust the other. You can lose control with me just as easily as you take it from me."

Gareth stared at her for a long moment, then his arms came around her and he drew her against his chest with a contented sigh. But as Beatrice closed her eyes and began to slip into sleep, she couldn't help but be troubled that Gareth hadn't responded to her statement. Although they would be married and she did trust him with her body and her future, she didn't know if *he* could trust her enough to give himself to her as she did to him.

And the idea that she would be the only one surrendering left her feeling empty and vulnerable for the first time since she had given herself to the man who would soon be her husband.

Chapter Fifteen

$\mathcal{B}$eatrice slipped from Gareth's chamber and quietly shut the door behind her. A few days before she would have felt awkward leaving the room where she could be seen by any servant or even her sister or brother-in-law, but today she felt no shame or worry. All had been resolved between her and Gareth. There was nothing left to do but marry.

With a smile, she moved down the long stairway and the hallway to the dining room. As she neared the room, she heard sounds within the chamber. Her smile fell as she realized it was Ethan and Miranda whispering within, despite any attempts they made to muffle their voices. Though she couldn't make out the words, from their concerned tones it was clear her family still harbored trepidations about her relationship and future with Gareth.

She stared at the cracked door. It wasn't that she was a coward, but last night had been so wonderful that she didn't want to come down from the high that still pulsed through her. She didn't want to return to her usual role of explaining and defending herself to people who simply didn't understand her needs. Not like Gareth did.

She gathered up the hem of her skirt and scooted past the door to the foyer, being careful to be as quiet as she could so no one would hear her from within the dining room.

In a short time, Gareth would join her downstairs and together they could face her family. With him by her side, she was certain she would find the strength to make Ethan and Miranda understand her position.

Until then, she wanted to step outside and enjoy the fresh morning air. If nothing else, she hoped to prepare herself for what would surely be the final battle to come.

Outside there was a warmth to the morning that made Beatrice smile as she shut the door and moved down the drive to the grassy hills of the estate. In a few weeks, this would be her permanent home. That gave her a thrill, for it was a place where her mother couldn't control her and her sisters wouldn't judge her.

She sighed with contentment. Being here, knowing she would soon wed, was more than she had dared to hope for when she began this bargain with Gareth.

Except those things were not the only ones that made her smile. In truth, the time she had spent with him had made her forget the mercenary reasons she had come here with him and surrendered herself.

There was a story her father had read to her as a girl. A tale of a beauty asleep in a tower who could only be awakened by true love. At the time he read it to her, Beatrice had thought it rather silly that the girl would need a prince to wake her. But now . . .

Now she understood that fanciful tale all the better. Before Gareth *she* had been asleep. It had only been half a life for her in London, a sleep existence where she only functioned, but did not thrive. She had been waiting until Gareth had challenged her to want more, to accept more, to surrender all she had and more.

Like the beauty in the story, he had awakened her, although it was with a bit more than a mere chaste kiss.

She frowned as she crested a low hill and looked out over the estate grounds. The story had said love could awaken the girl. But she and Gareth didn't have that. Passion, yes. An understanding, most definitely.

But love?

For the first time in her life, Beatrice wondered if she would miss such a feeling. Would she come to long for it over time?

No. That was silly. She had never been bold or foolish enough to love any man. It would be unfair to demand it of Gareth now. They could have a good life together without such sentimental nonsense.

She began to turn back, hoping Gareth had already joined Miranda and Ethan for breakfast while she took her walk. Together they would face them and together they would convince them to accept the fact that they would be married. If they couldn't . . . well, the decision had been made, no matter what her family said.

But as she turned, her thoughts on the future, she suddenly felt a powerful pressure at her throat. A big, muscular arm latched around her, holding her against the hard, immoveable chest of a person she couldn't see.

"No!" she cried, but was cut off when a hand clamped a piece of cloth over her mouth. It smelled sickly sweet as it covered her nose and filled her throat with cloying scent. She struggled for a moment, but then her body turned heavy. Her eyes began to droop. She fought the feeling, but it was too powerful to deny.

And there was only darkness.

When Gareth entered the dining room to find only Ethan and Miranda Hamon awaiting him, he groaned inwardly. Although he and Beatrice had fully resolved their future last night and no amount of argument from her family would change their present course, he still did not look forward to the confrontation about to come.

"Good morning, my lord, my lady," he said with a tight smile.

Miranda returned the expression warily. "Good morning, Lord Highcroft."

Ethan hardly looked up from his tea except to glare at Gareth briefly. "Highcroft."

"I trust your rooms were comfortable," Gareth asked as he poured himself a cup of the steaming liquid. "And your view satisfactory."

Miranda nodded. "Yes. Your estate is very beautiful."

Gareth inclined his head as thanks. He had purposefully put the two in a room overlooking the finest part of his estate. He wanted them to see, however they could, that Beatrice would be comfortable here.

"Perhaps later we could all take a stroll down to the lake together," he suggested. "I'm certain my housekeeper could arrange for a luncheon for our party."

Ethan speared him with a superior glare. "I don't think Beatrice likes a picnic," he murmured. "She has never been fond of the outdoors."

Gareth arched a brow. A few days before, Beatrice had been quite *enthusiastic* about the outdoors. Just the thought made him smile.

"Perhaps she has simply never found the right outdoor activity to tempt her," he said softly.

When the two looked at him incredulously, he shrugged. "You two may not know Beatrice as well as you believe you do."

Miranda folded her arms, and in her eyes Gareth saw a spark rather like the one Beatrice possessed. No matter how loudly each would deny it, the sisters were more alike than they admitted.

"And *you* do, sir?" Lady Rothschild asked. "Simply because you have compromised her?"

Gareth wrinkled his brow.

"Since you bring up the indelicate subject, my lady, I am happy to reply. What is between us is much more than the mere physical. Your sister and I have formed a deeper bond than just that."

As he said it, Gareth realized just how true it was.

"Beatrice puts on a face to the world," he mused, almost more to himself than to the couple before him. "Yes, it is sometimes bitter and off-putting, but when one takes the time to look past that, one can see her reasons for being so protective of herself. In my time with her, I have found her to be quite intelligent, which interests me. And when she is treated properly, she is capable of much vulnerability and trust."

Miranda was staring at him now, almost as if he had said her sister had taken over a small country. She shook her head. "It is hard for me to picture that what you say is true."

"Because Beatrice has kept herself from you for so long," Gareth said with an arch of his brow. "But that doesn't mean that the feelings and thoughts you didn't see weren't present, my lady."

Miranda pursed her lips, but made no vocal argument.

Gareth continued, "I realize you have grave doubts about me, but if you acknowledge nothing else, at least admit that your sister has some sense. After so long searching for a husband, she would not pick unwisely."

"But it is the fact that she has waited so long that troubles us," Ethan Hamon interrupted. "You cannot deny that she has long kept herself at arm's length from any man who was interested. Why would she suddenly run to you?"

Gareth leaned back and eyed Lord and Lady Rothschild evenly. "You took her sister to the country, did you not? To match her? Leaving Beatrice alone with a mother who has done almost everything in her power to ruin her daughters' chances at marrying well."

When Miranda flinched, Gareth knew she was thinking of whatever she, herself, had endured at the hands of their troubled mother.

"I tried to explain—" she began.

"Why would your explanations mean anything to her?" Gareth interrupted. "In that emotional moment, all she could see was that she was being thrown aside, abandoned to old maidenhood and a life as your mother's companion. If that drove your sister to make a desperate bargain, it is only understandable."

"So you admit she was desperate when she turned to you," Rothschild said, rising to his feet in what could only be interpreted as a threatening stance.

Gareth didn't back down. "Initially, yes. But I would have been a fool not to consider her offer. Neither of us had much to ingratiate ourselves to the *ton*, so our prospects of making a marriage were slim at best. Why *not* see if we could have a reasonable match together? Beatrice came here to test our connection, but as soon as she arrived, her desperation began to fade. We *have* forged a bond, something that is likely stronger than most arranged marriages. And I think you can see that she would be taken care of here."

"But your past . . ." Miranda whispered, her voice breaking with worry.

Gareth flinched. It seemed he would never overcome the rumors about Laurel's death. And for the first time he cared about what he would lose if he continued to be viewed as a murderer.

"Why don't we ask Beatrice about that?" he suggested. "Where is she?"

Miranda wrinkled her brow. "I wouldn't know, my lord. We have yet to see her this morning. I assume she is still abed or perhaps readying herself for the day."

Gareth stepped forward. "No. She is not. She came down before I did."

The moment he said it, Ethan Hamon's face darkened and Gareth swallowed back a curse. He had revealed too much, leaving little doubt that he and Beatrice had spent the night together, but for the moment he didn't care. He was only concerned about Beatrice.

"We should find her."

Miranda shook her head at his shift of mood. "You seem worried. Could she not have simply returned to her chamber or been otherwise waylaid?"

Gareth nodded. "I suppose, but I would feel better if I knew her whereabouts for certain."

As he left the room, Ethan Hamon followed. "What is going on here, Highcroft? Either you wish to utterly control my sister-in-law or you have reason to fear for her safety. Neither is comforting to me. So which one is it?"

Gareth ignored his guest as he motioned for a servant who was standing at the end of the hallway.

"You there, did you see Miss Albright this morning?" he asked.

The young woman turned toward him with a shake of her head. "I'm sorry, sir, I didn't. But I believe the footman Bradley was out and about this morning doing a few errands."

"Fetch him," Gareth ordered, his tone sharp. "Immediately."

The girl scurried away and within a few moments, she returned with one of the younger footmen at her heels. "What is it, sir?"

"Did you see Miss Albright while you were carrying on your duties this morning?" Gareth asked.

After a moment of consideration, the footman nodded. "Yes, sir. I was outside drawing some water when I saw the young lady come out the front door. She took a walk down the path, but after that I didn't see her."

Gareth froze. He had told Beatrice not to wander the estate grounds alone, not after the attack from his late wife's brother.

"You didn't see her return?" he asked.

"No, sir."

"You two go back and determine if anyone else saw her come back to the house, and do it quickly," Gareth snapped. "I'll go and search the grounds myself."

Both servants looked at him with clear concern, but didn't argue as they fled to question the others in the house. Once they were gone, Gareth grabbed for the door, but before he could, Ethan Hamon caught his wrist.

"Enough. Tell me what is going on. Why are you so worried about Beatrice?"

"Follow me," Gareth said as he shook off the other man's hand. "I'll explain everything while we look for her."

With that, he was out the door with Miranda and Ethan close behind. He scanned the estate grounds from the doorway then began down the path that led to the rolling hills and trees in the distance.

While they hurried, Gareth explained what had happened just a few days before, when Beatrice had been attacked by the brother of his late wife. And the threats the other man had made against her life.

"What the hell is wrong with you?" Ethan Hamon said as he grabbed for Gareth's arm and hauled him around to face him. "You should have told us this immediately upon our arrival! If my wife's sister was being threatened, I had a right to know. To protect her from that other person, from *you* and what your past has wrought!"

Gareth pulled himself free. There was no sign of Beatrice anywhere and the longer she was gone without word, the more afraid he grew for her. So Rothschild's accusations stung all the greater.

"I didn't fucking kill my wife," he burst out. Then he stopped. Until he had confessed that to Beatrice, he hadn't told anyone else. His silence was atonement, punishment.

But now he wanted Miranda and Ethan to know the truth. To hear it from his own lips. He wanted a chance at a life again . . . with Beatrice.

"It doesn't bloody well matter, does it?" Ethan snapped. "*Someone* believes you did, and they might be willing to hurt Beatrice in some twisted quest for revenge."

"Stop it, stop it, both of you!"

Both men turned to find Miranda standing a few feet away from them. Her eyes were wide and wild, rimmed with tears. And in her trembling fingers she held a slipper.

"This is my sister's," she whispered and one of her tears glided down her cheek. "I recognize it, for we had a row over her expensive taste when she brought these slippers home."

Gareth snatched the shoe from Miranda's grasp, staring at the delicate brocading and expensive stitching. There was no way Beatrice would play Cinderella games with him. Someone had taken her and with enough force that she had lost her shoe in the process.

He turned toward Ethan. "Please, please help me," he whispered, and scarcely recognized his own trembling voice. "Please help me find her."

Ethan nodded. "Do you know where she might be?"

"We should speak to my former brother-in-law," he said softly. "He was once a reasonable man, if he has her perhaps we can negotiate her return."

Ethan pulled his wife into his embrace and briefly held her as he whispered, "Go back to the house, Miranda."

She pulled away. "No! I want to——"

"Please," he said sharply. "You need to be there in case she makes her own way home. And to call for the magistrate. Please do this for me, and for her."

A world of communication moved between husband and wife, and Gareth turned away from it. He and Beatrice shared the same silent understanding. The difference was that while Miranda and Ethan clearly knew the love the other felt for them, Gareth had never told Beatrice that he cared. That she was more than a sexual plaything.

That he would die if he lost her.

And as he and Ethan hurried toward the stables to get horses, Gareth prayed that he would be in time to tell Beatrice all that and more.

Chapter Sixteen

As Beatrice came awake, it was through a strange fog. As if she were caught between darkness and reality, she fought troubled dreams to open her eyes. She *had* to open her eyes, though she wasn't certain why such urgency accompanied that floating thought.

After a while, the clouds in her mind cleared. She was welcomed back to the world by stomach-rolling nausea, intensified by a sickly sweet taste that lingered in her mouth. The taste, coupled with the utter darkness in the strange room around her brought back, with terrifying clarity, the details of her abduction.

She had hoped that it was all a dream, but now, lying at an odd angle on a hard floor, feeling the pounding in her head that had been brought on by whatever drug had rendered her unconscious, there was no denying what had happened.

She had been taken, though she had no sense of when it had happened. It could have been moments, it could have been days.

As she came to all those realizations, her eyes began to adjust to the room around her and she realized it wasn't entirely dark, as she had originally thought. There was a dim light in the corner, blocked by something so that it hardly pierced the haze.

In the hopes she could see better, she moved, but was instantly rewarded by a sharp pain in her arms. They had been tied behind her back. Panic clawed at her, but Beatrice fought the weak emotion. There was no time for such foolishness now. Calm and calculated plans were her best . . . and perhaps her *only* hope.

She shifted, trying to scoot herself into a seated position, both to better find her bearings and perhaps ultimately mount an escape. But as she began to slide, she heard a low chuckle from across the room. She froze. It seemed she wasn't alone after all. Her captor was present.

"Hello?" she called out, trying to keep her fear from her voice. "Who's there?"

There was no response and she barely held back a frustrated moan. Her intuition told her that this was no accidental taking—not a robbery for money or ransom. No, whoever had taken her was playing a game, enjoying the knowledge that she was at his mercy, toying with her.

She rolled onto her stomach and turned her face. The floor was dirty, she felt dust and rough wooden planks against her cheek. How she wished she was at home. With Gareth. Why hadn't she simply faced her sister and Ethan?

She drew in a deep breath. No. She wouldn't think of that now. Her energy had to be spent on getting out, and first she had to know who had taken her. There was only one person she could think of: the same man who had attacked her a few days before.

If he was so bold as to approach her on Gareth's estate, it stood to reason that he might return again looking for her. He had, after all, spoke of revenge.

She shivered as she thought of the anger in that other man's eyes . . . the mad despair. He was Gareth's former brother-in-law . . . *Adam*, she remembered Gareth had called him. In his grief over his sister's death, it seemed he had lost his sense. But that didn't mean he didn't still have decency. And if she appealed to that, perhaps she could talk her way free.

"Adam?" she called through the darkness. When her voice trembled, she swallowed against the dryness and spoke again, "Adam, you don't want to hurt me."

"Adam? That fool doesn't have the stomach, no matter how much damning evidence he is given," came the voice from the corner in return. It was laced with annoyance.

Beatrice's heart leapt with pure fear at the realization that she didn't know who had taken her after all. Although the voice seemed familiar, she couldn't place it and she certainly couldn't think of anyone besides Adam who knew she was with Gareth, let alone would take her.

"Who are you?" she asked, turning to anger to mask her fear. "How dare you!"

There was a long silence and then a screech of a chair being dragged across wood. She winced and when she opened her eyes the light in the room was suddenly bright. She craned her neck to see and was shocked when a man suddenly loomed over her.

Although his face was twisted in an emotional mask, there was no doubt that it was Gareth's footman. The one who seemed to hate her. Hodges, she remembered was his name.

"Y—you . . ." she murmured, utterly confused.

"Yes, my dear," he drawled and he slowly turned his face to look at her more closely. He smiled, mocking and cruel. "You weren't expecting me, I wager."

"No," she said with a scowl. "Release me at once."

His smile faltered. "Always the bitch, aren't we? Always the 'higher than thou' *lady*. Except you made yourself a whore quickly enough."

Beatrice flinched at the harsh words, but she refused to break eye contact with the bastard who towered over her. "Perhaps I did, but I am Lord Highcroft's whore. And you shall suffer his wrath if you do not let me go."

Hodges's hand darted down and he grasped her collar. With a painful wrench, he yanked her to her feet and gave her a hard shake. With her hands bound, she was helpless against the assault and could only bite back a cry of pain as her aching shoulders strained.

"Don't you understand?" he barked into her face. His breath stank of whiskey and tobacco as little flecks of spittle hit her turned cheek. "You are suffering *my* wrath. And so will he before I am finished."

He pushed her back and she stumbled onto her backside. She blew out a breath of air as her shoulder popped. Lightning-hot pain rushed through her body and she nearly blacked out, but somehow maintained consciousness as she slid as far away from him as the small room would allow.

She was hurt now, though she didn't know how badly. All she was certain of was that the injury put her at a disadvantage if she got the opportunity to fight or run. And if the sadistic bastard who had taken her found out . . . well, he would probably delight in using it to torture her.

She fought back a moan as the pain in her shoulder throbbed ceaselessly. Focus. She had to focus.

"Why?" she whispered, removing the agony from her voice as best she could. "Why would you have so much anger toward me when you have only known me a short time. Is this because I was impolite to you when I arrived at the estate?"

He smiled. "I admit, it is an added pleasure and so much easier to punish such a wretched girl, but in the end my vengeance has nothing to do with you."

She shook her head. "Then why?"

"*Him.*"

As he said the word, Hodges's face twisted and there was so much hatred and brutal anger in his expression that Beatrice froze in the face of it. In that one look, she saw all the torture and torment he intended to visit upon her before he ultimately ended her life. And she had no doubt that he *would* extinguish her life eventually.

"You want to punish Gareth," she whispered.

He nodded. "Indeed I do."

"He has been a difficult master," she said, forcing her tone to be soft, even submissive. Perhaps if he saw her as an ally, he could be convinced to end his plans.

He locked gazes with her and there was disgust on his face. "Of course not. For that we spit in your soup, we piss in your laundry. No, to warrant this kind of retribution, a man has to do something far worse."

"What did he do?" she asked.

"He killed the woman I loved," he spat.

Beatrice couldn't help but recoil at those words. "Who—"
She broke the question off as she thought of the only woman Gareth had ever been accused of harming. Her eyes widened as she stared up at her captor.

"Laurel?" she asked.

"Don't say her name," he barked as his hand came back in a striking motion.

Beatrice turned her face, bracing her body for his fist, but it didn't come. When she opened her eyes and looked at him, he was clenching his fingers open and shut as he stared down at her with a menacing madness that frightened her to her very core.

"Not yet," he murmured, almost to himself rather than to her. "If I start, I won't be able to stop."

She couldn't help but gasp out a tear-filled sound that summed up all her fear, all her regret.

"You loved her," she sobbed, forgoing all pretense of haughty anger or irritation that normally defined her reactions.

He nodded once, and beyond the lunacy of his revenge she saw how truly broken a man this person was. What he said was true, at least to him.

"I did. And she loved me. She was carrying my child the night Highcroft caused her death." He slammed a hand against the table beside him. "He took *everything* from me that night."

She winced at the violence of the action. "I'm sorry."

"Not yet," he murmured as he moved toward her. "But you will be. The Marquis of Highcroft robbed me, raped me, he murdered some part of me when Laurel died. Now I will do the same to him over as long a time as I can manage."

When Gareth kicked open the front door to his former brother-in-law's worn-down home, it brought a handful of ragged servants running. But one look at the two powerful men who stepped into the foyer and no one made any motion to come closer or stop their advance.

"Where is your master?" Gareth cried, barely holding in his anger, his fear, all the emotions when he thought of Beatrice being kidnapped. "Where is Adam Branden?"

The servants all stared, silent, but finally a butler moved forward. "H–he is in his study, my lor—"

Gareth didn't wait for him to finish. He bolted down the hallway with Ethan close at his heels. But as he reached for the door, Ethan caught his arm.

"If you kill him, you won't find Beatrice," Ethan growled. "I understand your panic, but you must think of saving her, not of your revenge. Not yet."

Gareth shook off the other man's hand with a glare, but he took a deep breath. Rothschild was correct, as much as he would like to ignore his words and simply rip Adam to shreds. He needed the man alive and coherent if he was to uncover where he had taken Beatrice.

And if she was even still alive.

He shuddered at the thought and then pushed the door open. As the two men came into the darkened chamber, Gareth looked around. It had been so long since he had been in this house. Even before Laurel's death, he hadn't visited her family, hating their accusatory stares and the angry inter-actions that ultimately ensued when he spent more than a few moments with them.

What he saw gave him a shock. How far they had fallen,

even since his last visit. The room was shabby and had a dank feel to it that made Gareth shiver.

And then he saw his former brother-in-law. Adam sat in the dark at his desk, a bottle before him. He hadn't even looked up when the door opened, though Ethan and Gareth had made plenty of noise in the hallway.

"You—" Gareth began, but Ethan caught his arm and held him steady.

"Look at him," Rothschild whispered. "Whether he took Beatrice or not, the man is not right. If you attack him, you'll get nothing. Calm yourself."

Gareth clenched his teeth. "Adam," he finally managed to grind out.

The man at the desk looked up, jolting as if he were startled when he saw the two men at his door. Slowly, he rose and moved toward them.

"Highcroft?" he asked, tilting his head in confusion. "What are you doing here? Who is this?"

Ethan stepped forward and extended his hand slowly. "I am the Earl of Rothschild, Mr. Branden. And we have come here on very important business. My sister-in-law is missing."

Gareth leaned forward, staring at Adam and looking for any indication of guilt or remorse or even pride. But there was nothing. Adam was completely blank; no emotion whatsoever lined his face. It was almost unnatural.

"I don't know what you mean," Adam said.

Gareth couldn't take it anymore. With a yell, he leaped

across the room and caught Adam by the lapels. Dragging him across the desk, he threw the man down to the ground and straddled him, holding him still as he breathed through his nose like a noisy bull.

"You know exactly the fuck what we mean. You attacked Beatrice and threatened her. Do you think me so stupid that I wouldn't suspect you took her when she went missing?"

Adam blinked as if the violence had awoken him from a dreamlike state. He looked from Gareth to Ethan with confusion.

"The—the woman?" he asked. "Yes, I did approach her. I . . . I wasn't thinking. I meant her no harm, I only wanted to frighten her."

Gareth slammed the other man down harder against the floor. "Where is she? I swear to God, I will kill you now if you have harmed her."

"Stop," Ethan barked as he grabbed Gareth's shoulders and tugged. But Gareth didn't let go, and dragged Adam with him as they fell backward.

"Tell me," he shouted, full in Adam's face. "Where is she?"

His former brother-in-law shook his head and for the first time Gareth saw the full light of comprehension in Adam's eyes.

"I did not take her, I swear to you. I regretted coming to your estate, doing what I did, saying what I said, the moment I ran away. I was confused, and Hodges was so vile in his descriptions, in his statements about what I should do . . ."

Gareth stared as Adam continued to ramble. Finally, he lifted a hand. "Wait, wait. Did you say Hodges?"

Adam nodded. "He told me you had brought a new woman to your estate. A woman you intended to marry. He played into my pain and grief—"

"My *footman*, Hodges?" Gareth repeated as he shoved Adam away from him and staggered to his feet. "Are you saying he had something to do with why you came to my home? That he told you about Beatrice?"

Adam nodded, though he remained seated on the floor, seemingly oblivious to his odd position. "Yes."

"But . . . why?" Gareth asked, utterly confused. "Why would my servant do that?"

Adam looked at him with a shake of his head. "Didn't you know? Hodges and Laurel were . . . they had an affair."

Gareth staggered back, scrubbing a hand through his hair as he paced away across the room. His stomach turned at the thought, the concept that while Laurel flinched away from his touch, she had accepted a servant's without hesitation. And worse, that her relationship with that man had now put Beatrice in danger.

And his own ignorance that a wolf lived in his very midst had only made her situation worse.

"Do you think this Hodges to be so bold as to take Beatrice?" Ethan asked quietly from behind Gareth.

Gareth spun to face Adam.

The other man stared for a moment and then he slowly nodded. "When the child died, he went crazy."

"The child?" Gareth cried, his mind spinning. "Are you saying Laurel was pregnant when she died?"

Adam winced, but then nodded. "Hodges claimed it to be so."

Gareth's knees threatened to buckle. He and his wife had not had relations for long enough before her death that he doubted any child she might have carried would have been his. If Hodges believed Laurel to be pregnant . . . if he thought the babe to be his . . .

Well, that was more than enough motive for the worst kind of revenge.

"But why would he wait so long?" Gareth murmured. "He had two years to murder *me* in my bed."

Adam shrugged. "He didn't want to kill you without breaking you first. He's been plotting for two years and going steadily mad. The idea that you might marry again seemed to push him over the edge."

"So Hodges encouraged *you* to seek vengeance against Beatrice in order to hurt me," Gareth whispered.

"And when I refused after our last encounter, he was enraged." Adam shook his head. "He was out of control; nothing I could say would soothe him."

"Then he *could* have taken her," Ethan mused, meeting Gareth's eyes. Gareth saw pity there, worry that was almost as deep as his own.

Stomach turning, Gareth whispered, "Adam, you must tell me where he might have taken her. Her life could depend on it."

He knew it was a risk, talking about life and death with this man who had lost a most beloved sister. But after a long moment, Adam nodded.

"There has been enough death, enough pain," he whispered. "There is one place he might have gone . . ."

Chapter Seventeen

$\mathcal{B}$eatrice squeezed her eyes shut and a tear trickled from the corner of her eye to splash against the dusty floor. How long would it take for someone to miss her?

Miss her.

She almost laughed, though nothing about her situation was amusing in the least. After all the years she had spent since her father's death creating a wall around herself, blocking out any friendship or love . . . well, now she would pay. No one would care once she was gone. Beyond the juicy gossip such a gruesome end would garner, there would be little mourning, little regret. She feared even her family would feel more relief than loss.

And it was no one's fault but her own. Her actions had made her a pariah. They were the reason why no one would come for her.

Despair overcame her and she let the tears fall silently as she mourned her life, mourned all the things she should have done, mourned . . .

"Gareth," she whispered, low enough that Hodges wouldn't hear.

Gareth had seen past her protective barriers. He had forced her to face herself, her past. Gareth *would* come for her. Only he would be too late.

She forced her eyes open and looked across the dim room. In the distance, Hodges stood at a table. She couldn't see what he was doing, but occasionally she heard the slide of metal on metal, as if he was sharpening blades.

The footman would torture her. That much was clear. Even if he hadn't already told her, she had seen it in his eyes. She had heard it in his voice. Yet somehow it wasn't the pain that she feared or regretted. The closer she got to what she knew would be the end, the more she was saddened.

Saddened by the fact that Gareth would know she had suffered. When he saw her, it would surely break him and wrack him with guilt that he hadn't protected her.

And more than that, she felt overwhelmed by regret. Why had she resisted Gareth's desires for so long? Why had she kept herself from him in any way? And why hadn't she told him how she felt about him?

That she loved him.

When that thought pierced the hazy terror in her mind she almost cried out in pure pain. For so long she had fought to keep everyone and everything out and away, to protect herself. And now, *now*, when her heart was so clear to her that there was no question about how she felt, she was about to lose everything.

"Do you think I can't hear you whimpering?" Hodges snapped as he slammed his fist against the table before him. The old wood creaked beneath the force and Beatrice tensed as she readied herself for pain.

"Isn't that what you want?" she asked. "Isn't my suffering part of your sick plan?"

He chuckled as he turned slightly toward her. "Sick plan. How can you call me sick when you have actually enjoyed the games that Highcroft demands his women play? The servants can hear you moaning like a whore in his bed, you know."

"He never forced me, he never hurt me," she hissed, determined to defend Gareth to this bastard.

Hodges turned to pick up a thin blade from the collection of devices on the table. "So you liked what he did to you, you dirty harlot. You may have enjoyed his games, but trust that you won't like mine."

Beatrice pushed herself to a seated position, despite the stabbing pain her shoulder injury created. She shoved herself back, scooting toward the wall as Hodges advanced on her, step by slow step. He was smiling, viciously enjoying her fear, and she couldn't keep herself from expressing it with one, bloodcurdling scream as he lifted the blade over his head in preparation to slice through her skin.

But before he could do it, before he could maim her, kill her, the door behind him flew open. Beatrice screamed again as a blur of activity began. Hodges was pulled away from her, thrown across the room with enough force that the window by the door shattered when he hit the wall. Bright sunlight flooded the chamber.

Beatrice struggled to see what was happening in the confusion. When her eyes adjusted, she saw Gareth straddling the now prone footman, beating his fist into Hodges's face over and over again. He would kill him if he hadn't already. Ethan stood over the men, trying to stop Gareth, but unable to in the face of Gareth's rage.

"Gareth," Beatrice called out weakly.

Her voice stopped him mid-punch. Slowly he turned and the haze of anger that had darkened his face and turned him into a man she didn't know faded. He threw aside the limp body of the man who had taken her and crossed the room to her in three long strides.

"Beatrice," he whispered as he dropped to his knees before her. "God, I'm sorry."

He enfolded her in his arms and all the fear she had experienced, all the regrets that had made her ache, spilled free as she sobbed into his shoulder.

She was vaguely aware of hands untying her, probably Ethan's, since Gareth never released her. As she continued to cry, Gareth lifted her and cradled her to his chest as he carried her from the dingy little shack where she had been held.

"She's injured," Beatrice heard through her tears. Ethan's voice, and he sounded so concerned . . . so loving that her sobs came faster. "I'll fetch the magistrate and a vehicle to carry her home."

Slowly, her sobs subsided and Beatrice lifted her face from Gareth's shoulder to look up at him. He was staring down at her, his green eyes intense with emotion.

"Beatrice," he whispered. "I love you. I love you, do you hear me? I love you."

She was overwhelmed, washed away by the emotions of all she had endured and by the utter joy of hearing Gareth's confession. She opened her mouth, intent on confessing her own heart, but no words would come. The pain of her shoulder was too intense, her emotions too sharp.

So she settled her face back into his shoulder and let darkness take her again.

Gareth stood in the corner of his chamber, arms folded, watching silently as the doctor fussed over Beatrice. At least she was awake again. When she had collapsed into a faint he had been terrified that her life was close to an end, but the doctor reassured him it was only pain and high emotion that had brought her to that state.

Now she sat in his bed, propped up on white pillows, her blond hair around her shoulders, one of which was bandaged, her arm gathered close to her chest in a sling. The bastard who had taken her had dislocated it.

But it would heal. *She* would heal, the doctor insisted.

"There is nothing I despise more than fainting women," Beatrice snapped. "Except, perhaps, fawning doctors."

The doctor scowled at her, but Gareth couldn't help but smile. Beatrice's return to her normal, prickly self was the first indication that she wasn't permanently harmed by what she had endured.

Miranda, who was sitting beside her sister on the edge of the bed, shook her head. "He is only trying to help, dearest."

Beatrice rolled her eyes, but then her gaze darted to Gareth. When their gazes met, he saw what a front her attitude was. Unshed tears still shone in her stare. She was fragile, even if no one else could see it.

He moved forward. "Is that all, Doctor?"

The physician turned toward him. "Yes, though I do have a few instructions."

He motioned to the door. "Give them to her sister. Outside. I wish for all of you to leave us."

Miranda was on her feet in an instant, her eyes wide and outraged. "Absolutely not! I will not leave my sister—"

Before she could finish, her husband stepped toward her, laying a hand on her shoulder.

"Miranda," Ethan said softly.

That one word stopped her. She glanced briefly at Beatrice. Beatrice nodded slightly and Miranda frowned, but then she moved toward the door where a moment before, the doctor had departed muttering to himself in disapproval.

When they were alone, the door closed, Gareth turned toward Beatrice again. In her face, he saw her weakness, her softness, her vulnerability. But he also saw her strength. Not the kind that made her difficult and what others called a shrew, but something more.

"May I get you anything?" he asked, suddenly awkward.

She held his gaze for a long time before she shook her head slightly.

He moved toward her, hesitant as a bridegroom who had never lain with his bride. Because, despite all the physical pleasures they had shared, this was uncharted territory for him. He had never loved a woman. Now he felt uncertain of what to do.

"I—I said something to you when I found you," he said softly.

She squeezed her eyes shut and a little shiver rocked her. "Your emotion was high, Gareth, I know that. I wouldn't hold you to words you said in that moment."

He stared at her. "You think I didn't mean what I said to you?"

She swallowed hard and her blue eyes came open slowly. "Did you?"

He nodded as he moved toward her. He caught one hand, careful not to jostle her injured arm.

"I meant them with all my heart, Beatrice," Gareth whispered. "Dear God, I have never said such a thing to anyone before. Do you understand what I'm saying?"

Her lips parted slightly. "You love me?"

He nodded. "With everything I am, with everything I want to be. I love you."

She pulled her hand from his, but it was only to lift it to his cheek. With tears streaming down her face, she touched him, cupping his chin, stroking his cheek.

"Do you know what I thought of when I believed that man . . . Hodges . . . would kill me?"

Gareth shook his head slowly, trying not to be overwhelmed with anger at the thought of her torment. "No."

"I thought of *you*," she whispered. "I thought of how sad I was that I would never get to tell you how much I appreciated that you fought to see me for who and what I really am. And how much I love you."

Drawing back a fraction, Gareth stared at her. He knew Beatrice, he knew why she shied away from emotions, from dependence on any other person. Her frank honesty, her open emotion, those things meant the world to him. They were special gifts, things she did not readily share.

"You love me?" he whispered.

"With everything I am, with everything I want to be," she repeated his earlier words with a slow nod. "And you are certain you love me, even though I am difficult . . . a shrew?"

Gareth couldn't help but grin. His joy was too intense, too powerful not to show. "You are so much more than that, Beatrice. Even if no one else ever sees it, *I* see it. I see you and your heart."

Now she smiled. A broad, happy expression that lightened her face and made her even more beautiful to him. "What am I?"

He cupped her chin and moved in for a kiss. "Mine. You are mine."

And as he brought his lips to hers, she whispered, "Always."

Epilogue

Five Years Later

Beatrice watched as her twin sons raced down the hill, their chubby, toddler legs barely keeping them upright as they struggled to keep up with their older cousins, the children of Penelope and Winifred. The children's shrieks of laughter floated up from below and brought a smile to her face before she turned back to her family.

The sisters all sat together, enjoying their children and the bright sun of a summer's mid-morning. The only one missing from their gathering was their mother.

Beatrice frowned. It had been a year since Dorthea passed on, peacefully in her sleep. Despite all the trouble their mother had caused, Beatrice still found herself missing her.

After all her daughters were married, Dorthea had actually calmed slightly.

And as the grandchildren arrived, she had become even happier, loving them with a full acceptance she had never been capable of giving her own girls. All the Albright daughters appreciated that and often commented on Dorthea as time passed.

Blinking back tears, Beatrice let her gaze fall to each sister. Time and children had not lessened any of their beauty. The jealous harpies of the *ton* complained of it endlessly and nothing gave Beatrice more pleasure.

Miranda glowed as she rested her hand on the swell of her belly. After years of painfully unsuccessful trying, she was nearing the end of her first confinement.

"Are you well?" Beatrice asked softly when her sister exhaled a breath softly.

Winifred and Penelope both stopped their quiet conversation and turned toward their eldest sister. All of them had been worried about Miranda in the last nine months. After seeing her struggles, it was difficult not to be.

But Miranda laughed. "I'm very well. But I think you had better send one of the men for the doctor, as I believe this little one is finally ready to join his cousins."

Winifred was on her feet first. "I'll send Milo right away."

Penelope was fast on her heels. "And I'll have Jeremy stand by with Ethan. You know he'll be impossible until he knows you and the babe are well."

Once the two other sisters were gone, Miranda turned on Beatrice with a smile. "How did you know?"

She shrugged. "I saw it in your eyes."

Miranda held her gaze for a long time and Beatrice let her. For so long, she would have flinched away from her sister's regard, but now . . . after years of feeling just how right and powerful love could be, she no longer feared her own vulnerability. And while the *ton* might still call her a bitch behind her back, and perhaps she took some pleasure in acting the part, her family no longer steered away from her wrath.

For that she was very glad.

The terrace doors flew open and Ethan stepped out, his eyes wide and his expression utterly terrified. Behind him stood Jeremy, Penelope and Gareth. Even after all these years, Beatrice's heart still leaped as her husband met her gaze.

"It's time?" Ethan asked, his tone breathless and tense with anxiety. Beatrice rolled her eyes. Before the day was over, the men would likely have to get him drunk to keep him from having an apoplexy.

Miranda got to her feet slowly. "Indeed. Will you take me upstairs?"

Ethan caught her arm and they moved slowly inside, with Penelope and Jeremy close behind. Beatrice smiled as her own husband stepped out and put his arms around her.

"You look happy," he whispered.

She slipped her arms around his waist. "I am happy, *my lord*," she whispered. "I am here with you, with my family. I have everything I could ever want. How could I be anything but happy?"

He kissed her gently before they turned toward the hill where the children played. The place where she belonged.

Jess Michaels

Although **JESS MICHAELS** came to romance novels later in life than most, she always knew what she liked: ultra-sexy, emotional reads. Now she writes them from her purple office in central Illinois. She lives with her high school sweetheart husband and two support-ive cats. Readers can contact her at www.jessmichaels.com.